SHADOWS

OF THE FORGOTTEN

SHORE

AN IRISH GHOST STORY

ANGELA R. HUGHES

IMAGINE NOW PUBLISHING
www.angelarhughes.com

Editors Ashely White & Stephanie Cotta
Cover design by Erika Ryan
Images: Licensed Adobe Stock Photos, Canva.com
Illustrations by Millikodea

978-1-7362443-4-0   Paperback
978-1-7362443-5-7   Hardback
Library of Congress Control Number: 2025908254

Contents

A Guide to the Hidden Ones of Ireland

Throughout these pages, you will encounter creatures of Irish myth and folklore. Here is a brief guide to what they are and how to pronounce their names.

Balor (*BAH-lur*) – A monstrous king of the Fomorian giants, an ancient race of supernatural beings. Balor is said to have a deadly eye that brings destruction to all who fall under his gaze. He is also a reaper of souls, claiming the lives of those caught in his wrath.

The Gancanagh (*GAN-kah-nah*) – A male faery known as the "Love-Talker." He is a seductive and mischievous spirit who ensnares mortals with his charm, often leading them to ruin. The Gancanagh are also shapeshifters, able to take on different forms to better lure their victims.

Daoine Maithe (*DEE-nuh MAH-huh*) – Meaning "The Good People," this term refers to the fairies of Irish lore. Though they can be benevolent, it is wise to treat them with respect, for they are easily offended.

The Sluagh (*SLOO-ah*) – The restless, cursed dead who travel in dark flocks across the sky. These spirits seek out the dying, hoping to steal their souls and drag them away into the otherworld.

I dedicate this book to my grandmother, *Marjorie Ann Croan Gillmore*, whose home by the lake filled mine and my sisters' childhood with a lifetime of memories. I learned everything I would ever learn about playing cards from her. She was always up for a game with a cigarette between her fingers and coffee in her favorite mushroom mug. She never let me win without earning it fair and square.

I miss you, Grandma.

There was never a moment when you weren't happy to spend every waking second with me. Adventures were forever afoot in the forest's deer trails and muddy lake shores.

"I've heard it said more than once—
unforgiveness is like drinking poison and
expecting it to kill someone else. But that's not
how it works. The poison only *ever* harms the
one who drinks it."

The Shadow

"Gran, close the curtains," I called from upstairs, pulling my quilt up to my eight-year-old chin.

No answer.

These covers aren't thick enough. I'm still not safe. Whatever lurks outside my bedroom window—it's there. Waiting. Watching.

Demons prowl in the dark. Gran called them the *sluagh*, moaning spirits that flock like birds to herald one's death. Her eyes would grow wide as she'd warn, "If they call yer name, and ya listen too closely, they'll steal yer soul."

I swallowed the hard lump of fear choking me.

What do they look like? It's like they can see me but I can't see them.

Images of long spectral faces with wide mouths ready to devour me invaded my mind.

My mom called them wraiths sent by the demon king *Balor*—his eye of death—like the lighthouse outside my west-facing window. His ever-seeking eye spent its nights searching for souls to cast down into its pit of hellish giants.

"It's just an Irish bedtime story," Mom always said.

But that's not the truth. No, the sluagh were there, staring at me, even now. Their eyes bore through the window and onto my skin. I didn't dare open the curtains.

The wind howled, elevating my terror. "Gran!"

Her footsteps creaked up the stairs. She appeared over the steps with her hands on her hips and a perturbed grimace curling her lips. "Nora, don't be ridiculous," Gran said. She secured the sheer white curtains shut. I breathed a deep sigh of relief.

The drapes barely covered the large windows situated above my bed's headboard that overlook the sea. They were never a protection against my fear, but it *was* better with them closed.

"Please, Gran, can I sleep with you in your bed?" Falling asleep alone in my upstairs bedroom turned me inside out. Mom, Dad, Gran, and Grandad all slept in the bedrooms downstairs—too far away to keep me safe from the bogeyman that lurked in the shadows.

Gran huffed, shaking her head. "No, dear. You'll be just fine. Close yer eyes and say yer prayers, so Saint Mary can protect ya." She fondled the rosary beads around her wrist. Her eyes turned troubled, and her forehead pinched as she gazed out the small crack through the curtains.

Is she okay? Is this about earlier?

My mind replayed the horrifying conversation I'd overheard while clearing the dinner table. Gran and Mom had spoken in hushed voices that perked my curious ears. I wish I'd never overheard them talking about Gran's deceased younger sister. The scary thoughts of her death flooded my head.

I removed the covers from my face. "Gran, was it the sluagh that got her?"

"Hm?" Gran blinked and returned her gaze to me.

I gripped my quilt tighter. "Your sister . . . Great Aunt Neive."

"No, dear." She shook her head, then peered at her hands. "Neive was taken in by the wiles of a *gancanagh*. If my da would've been around, it wouldn't have been left up ta me ta keep her safe." Her lips tightened into a bitter line. "Off drinkin' wit' his mates when he should've been home wit' his gurls. She was so young. Only sixteen."

"What is a gancanagh?" I asked, pulling the sheets higher. My dark frizzy curls covered my face, only leaving enough room for my eyes.

"Oh, it's a beautiful *daoine maithe*."

A gasp caught in my throat. "A faery?"

Gran pressed her lips tighter and nodded. "The shapeshifter kind that can appear as cats—even human men." She leaned closer. "Handsome and alluring. My sister was deceived by one, and she became marked." Gran peered back toward the sea. "That's when Balor's eye saw her. I wish I could've protected her. Instead, I damned us all."

Balor's eye?

"What? Gran, no—"

"Oh," she interrupted, as though realizing I was frightened. "Ya have nothing ta fear, dearie. Yer too young." She touched her forehead and made the sign of the cross, kissing her rosary when she finished. "The Lord protects ya, love. The Lord protects ya." She kissed my freckled nose. "You go ta sleep now."

Gran patted my thigh, then got up to leave the room. Every part of me wanted to run for the door as my grandmother turned to close it behind her. Her fingers still on the handle, I shouted, "Don't close the door!"

Gran hesitated, propped the door wider, then disappeared into the low-lit hallway. The creaking of her footfalls down the stairs dwindled away.

Fear sank its fangs in my belly, tightening my chest and stealing my breath. That same fear kept me from dashing out of bed and after Grandma.

It might get me if I move.

What was it? One of Gran's monsters? Or maybe something else? It didn't matter. It was there. I was certain of it, and Gran had left me behind, and taken her rosary with her.

I thrust my quilt over my head. Sweat beaded down my neck and shivers crawled up my spine.

My breath tremored, alone, in that upstairs bedroom. I listened in terrified silence for any movement in the dark. The wind's eerie bale wailed from outside. The rushing sea waves were curling fingers, clawing ever closer from the shore. The settling house creaked a warning—I was not alone.

Gran failed to protect Aunt Neive. How could she possibly keep me safe?

Sometime within the late hours, when I couldn't keep my eyes open, I fell asleep. In the morning, when the lights were bright, and the sun blazed over the sea's horizon, I was new again. No more fear of monsters. Balor and his demons, who hovered above the sea outside Gran's windows, were gone.

I laughed at my fear as Grandad's morning radio show echoed up the stairs. A hot breakfast of rashers and eggs soon followed. The smell, an irresistible invitation, propelled me from my bed, and I scrambled my way down the stairs.

Gran always sat at the table with her crossword, sipping coffee from her favorite mug, detailed with seventies-style green, orange, and yellow mushrooms—a cigarette teetering between her fingers, its smoke curling toward the coned pendant light above.

We started every morning this way. The illusion of terrors faded with the night . . . until bedtime came once more. Those dark spirits, and gods of the sea, were phantoms that came and went.

But the sluagh did come. The demons took Gran when I was twelve. We moved away from Carraig Brón to Chicago in a matter of weeks. The distance should have kept the monsters at bay, but it hadn't. Nothing could stop the spirits from taking my mom ten years later. The cursed phantoms called her name, and I couldn't stop it.

1

Flight Back Home

10 Years Later

"Listen to me, Nora," my dad chided in an unempathetic, strictly business tone as we sped down the highway toward the airport. "Returning back to school so soon isn't a good idea. Your mom's funeral was only two days ago. You need to give yourself time to grieve before throwing yourself back into your studies."

My lips tightened. The sound of my dad's voice grated in my head like nails on a chalkboard.

What does he know?

I bit my lip, holding in the rage that wanted to fly from my tongue. My dad didn't know the first thing about what I should be doing. One tear—only one tear fell from his eye as the minister spoke at Mom's funeral. He had just sat there with his perfectly polished dark hair, trim beard, and three-piece suit, as if made of stone.

Always the executive. Never the human being.

The heat that radiated off my face as he stood like a stoic statue while Mom's coffin was lowered into the ground still lingered.

"I prefer to be back at school with my friends," I growled,

glaring out the window. The blurred view of the city rushing past was a good distraction.

Only five more miles, and he'll be dropping me off at the airport.

I leaned my head against the car window, anticipating my escape back to a world where everything made sense.

My dad tsked. "I should just turn this car around and take you back home."

I whipped my head toward him. "Home?"

He sighed, rolling his eyes. "Yes, home."

"My home has *never* been"—I twisted my lips and spat out the next word with disgust—"*Chicago.*"

"Nora, when are you going to let that go? It was time for us to move on."

My fists clenched my jacket sleeve. "Move on?"

"Yes, Nora. You need to grow up already."

My face heated. "Grow up? You mean be like you?" I shook my head. "You have no idea what it did to pull me away from the only home I ever knew—with no explanation. No time to even say goodbye."

The leather on the steering wheel creaked as my dad's grip tightened. "I didn't owe an explanation to a twelve-year-old child."

Of course. He didn't owe me anything. Never has, never will.

I was twelve when Gran passed; Grandad had died a year earlier. That had been Dad's cue to pull us away from our home in Ireland and move us to Chicago. I had *no* say in the matter— and neither did Mom.

"We can't just leave," I'd screamed at him. "What about Declan?" But it was like he refused to hear me.

Chicago couldn't have been more different than our quaint home by the Irish coast.

"You never wanted anything to do with Mom's home

country—or the family that came with her. You were probably relieved once they passed."

A tense growl emanated from my dad's side of the car. "Nora, you stop right there. You have *no idea* what you're talking about."

"Oh really? Then fill me in. I'd like to know. I'm not twelve anymore."

My dad's lips pursed. The muscle in his jaw twinged as he glared forward, remaining silent.

I rolled my eyes at the ludicrous reality of it all. "And now you want me to stay here with you—without Mom? My bedroom isn't even mine anymore. It's crammed with your treadmill and boxes from your office." A flush of grief surged up my neck. My insides groaned, and I curled into my stomach. My bedroom had just been another sign that not only would Chicago never be home, but that Dad had not made the effort to make it home.

"We can fix your room. This was sudden for me too, Nora. She was healthy. She was . . ."

I'd never even heard of the disorder that killed Mom, but it also killed Gran. I believed Gran had died of a stroke for the last ten years.

But no. That's just what they'd led me to believe.

My stomach twisted in knots thinking about it, making it harder to control my tongue. "If you'd been paying attention, she'd still be alive."

"You do *not* get to blame me, Nora. Not for this."

Oh, but I do. If I had been there, I would have noticed. I would have taken her to the doctor.

I couldn't help but think it—and now I'd said it too. Every memory of Mom, and everything she touched, had become a spring-loaded trigger of pain, and my dad was at the center of it all.

"The headaches should've been enough for you to take

her to the doctor, but you were too busy. You're always too busy. You weren't paying attention. Too preoccupied golfing and eating lunch with your high-rise clients, while Mom stayed behind and did all your paperwork." My eyes started to fill with tears. I took a deep breath and forced them back.

Dad's body trembled, his knuckles turning white as he gripped the steering wheel. "If you want to blame me, *fine*. Make me the villain, Nora."

It was as if the marrow in Mom's bones dried out—now absent of what was necessary to keep her alive. The doctor said her death could have been prevented had the disease been caught.

Nice sentiment now that she's already dead.

"We need to fix this, Nora," Dad said, pulling off the highway and merging into the five-lane chaos of the airport.

I sniffed. "Fix what?"

"This thing between us."

Oh, now he cares about having a relationship with me?

I reached for the door handle, ready to get out as soon as we arrived at the departure terminal. Thoughts of home, of Gran, of being in the arms of someone who actually loved me, swirled in my head. Was there anyone who could understand just how deep of a hole I was falling into? Anyone that cared? Gran was dead. Mom was dead. I didn't want to go back to school, but—

I am not about to stay here with Dad.

He pulled the car over at the departure gate, where Delta Airlines awaited to take me back to Oregon. Far away from the fumes of the dingy Chicago metropolis, back to university, where the green trees and coastline were the closest I've come to home.

Home.

I clicked the handle and opened the door, but Dad reached for my arm, pulling me back to my seat.

"We are all the family we have left, Nors."

His words were like poison seeping into my ears. The trigger had been pulled. The explosion, like a gun telling me to run. But where? My dad couldn't be the only person left.

If he'd loved me—if he'd loved Mom—things would have been different. He would've wanted to "*fix this*" a long time ago.

My arm went still in Dad's grasp before I yanked it away. "No. You're the only family *I* have left. You have your brothers." Hot angry tears pooled in my eyes.

"Your mom wouldn't want you to leave like this," he said with what seemed like zero compassion.

I shut my eyes—rage pushing out the tears.

Manipulator.

"You owe it to her—and to me—to be bigger than this." His voice was cold and hard. "I have things to do—a business to run. You are too old to not consider how your choices affect others."

I gasped. "*My* choices?"

"You can't keep blaming me for everything bad that has happened in your life."

I huffed as heat flooded my veins. "You didn't love her. You don't love me." My head spun. "You let her die! You always have to control everything, except the things that actually matter—*don't you*? I don't need anything from you. And I certainly don't have anything left to give you."

I spared one last glance at his widening eyes, then burst out of the car and slammed the door shut. My feet stormed toward the back of Dad's Lexus. I flung my backpack over my shoulder and grabbed my suitcase before slamming the trunk shut.

I didn't turn around. I didn't say goodbye. I didn't even stop to check in with Delta. No—my feet moved on past. I wasn't going back to my university, but I wasn't staying in Chicago either.

I'm leaving this all behind.

"Welcome onboard Aer Lingus," the pilot's canned voice boomed overhead. "We are thrilled to have you traveling with us on this non-stop flight to Dublin. Our flight will be around seven hours, twenty-five minutes with an approximate arrival time of 16:35. So lay back, enjoy your flight, and turn your attention to the flight attendants for a brief presentation on airline safety."

My mind tuned out the attendant as she took her position at the center of the aisle. I rolled my eyes, and her voice disappeared. I pulled my headphones over my ears, still fuming about my fight with Dad. I stared out the window, the wing of the plane blocking my view as we prepared to roll down the turnpike.

I will not let him dictate how I live.

Maybe I should've flown back to Oregon, to school, and the only sense of normalcy I had left. But somehow, in a blur of madness, grief, or rebellion, I found myself taking out the credit card Dad had given me for emergencies and buying a ticket to go home. My real home.

It was sheer luck a flight to Dublin was set to leave not even an hour after I'd arrived at the airport. The rush to get through security and arrive at the gate in time had been a welcomed distraction, but now that the dust had settled and the flight was ready to take off, the sinking feelings returned.

Mom's gone. And Dad's just . . . I'm all I have left.

I exhaled and closed my eyes, relieved that the seat next to me remained vacant.

I wanted to be left alone. I couldn't breathe. I was, once again, being suffocated by a raging tornado of loss. Its black teeth gnawed on my insides. My mind, incapable of processing the shattering pieces that whipped around me.

Nothing would ever be the same again. No matter how much I wished it could be. Mom would never make her famous buttered ham and cheese sandwiches again. The trigger of loss pulled, and I gasped.

Hold it together. Don't cry.

I covered my mouth to keep the rising anguish inside. Luckily, the igniting, whirring engines of the airplane were loud enough to stifle any noise I made. I swallowed the pain back down as hard as I could.

My thoughts switched back to Dad. It was easier to be angry at him than to think about the fact that my mom was gone.

Forever. Gone forever.

I squeezed my eyes tighter. My mom's phantom hand reached for mine but vanished as the plane rattled, and my eyes shot back open.

The seat belt sign dinged and lit above my head. I grumbled while fastening the belt around my hips.

The stewardess tapped my seat. "Please lift your seat into an upright position."

I tried not to shoot her a snarky glare and instead forced a smile and lifted my seat. My phone buzzed in my pocket, signaling I'd received a text message.

Don't look. It won't be anything good.

I snuck a peek anyways before putting my phone in airplane mode.

(Dad) James Morrigan:
"Call me when you land."

I pursed my lips and clicked the screen off. Anger percolated in my chest.

I am not going to call you. If only you knew what I was really up to.

But he wouldn't know. I wouldn't tell him. Otherwise, he'd find some way to stop me. To stop the plane, even.

"I am not a child," I mumbled under my breath. I swallowed hard . . . It was his credit card I'd used to charge my ticket, though.

I'll be on my own soon enough. I'll disappear. I don't need him anymore, anyway.

I closed my eyes again as the plane started to roll forward. Soon I'd be breathing the salty, pure air of the village I grew up in. It would be within arm's reach in a matter of hours. "Carraig Brón," I whispered, a familiar nostalgia taking hold. It was far away from the cloggy, rancid air of Chicago.

Gran and Grandad's house was a white thatch home called after their surname, The Flaherty House. It overlooked the sea, with a view of Tóraigh Island and its lighthouse. Carraig Brón was a small tourist village not far from Donégal. I would catch a bus in Dublin as soon as I landed.

Maybe my friends are still there.

There were two boys my age I'd played with down by the shore. A swirl of nerves tightened my stomach.

They are probably at university like me. They likely wouldn't have stayed in that small village.

I was particularly fond of Declan. He and I—

I shook my head; the crushed look on his face was still burned into my mind from when I left. I didn't even have time to say goodbye. Dad had grabbed me by the arm and forced me into the car. Declan stared after me like a lost soul. "Just give me a chance to say goodbye," I'd cried. I still don't know why Dad hadn't let me. If he'd only given me a minute, maybe things could have been different. I will never forgive him for that.

I need to think about something else. Anything else.

The memory of Declan pulled on the already fragile edges of my heart, making it ache.

I'll get a room at Pete's Pub & Inn. I am sure it's still run by Don and Carla. Surely, they will remember me. Carla was Mom's close friend, and they were both friends of the family. Then, I'll go see Lem after I'm settled. Hopefully no one is renting out Gran and Grandad's house.

Lem, another family friend, owned the post office/bookshop in town, and took care of The Flaherty House as a vacation rental for my parents. My father always wanted to sell it, but because of Mom, he never did. Now that she was gone—

"Ugh," I dropped my head into my hands, massaging my temples. Another surge of grief hit my throat. The plane sped up, and we lifted off the ground. The pressure pushed me back against my seat, forcing tears from my eyes. I turned my head toward the window so the passengers in the seats across the aisle couldn't see me unraveling.

I wiped the tears away, but they just kept falling.

Maybe if we keep soaring higher, we'll meet Mom up there.

But we didn't. The plane levelled out, and the seat belt sign dinged again.

"We have now reached an altitude of thirty-five thousand feet," the captain announced throughout the cabin. "It should be smooth sailing from this point on; however, we may experience some turbulence later over the Atlantic."

"Turbulence," I grumbled.

As if I need any more of that in my life.

The captain went on, "Feel free to move about the cabin, but please keep your seat belt fastened while seated. The stewardesses will be bringing you refreshments shortly."

The captain's voice sobered me, and I was able to breathe again. I wiped my hot cheeks dry and took a long deep breath. No turning back now. My dad couldn't stop me.

I need to get there. I need to see it. My home.

2

Pete's Pub & Inn

I burst into the house, water dripping from my brunette curls and the hem of my clothes. My shoes and socks were soaked, so I tried to pull them off and hop upstairs before anyone noticed me.

"What're ya after? Look at the state of ya'!"

I glanced toward the kitchen, my shoulders tensing. My eyes widened in a silent plea, while my growing smile begged for forgiveness. Gran stood with one hand on her hip, a tea towel draped over her shoulder, and a cigarette balanced on her lip. A warm and distinct aroma greeted me. Gran's cinnamon biscuits . . . mixed with stale smoke.

She grabbed the cigarette from her mouth and blew out the smoke. "Out there wit' Declan again?"

I looked at the floor and nodded.

"The two of yous—again—swimmin' in the cold weather. In yer school uniforms no less. Yer mum will be furious."

"I d-didn' mean to, Gran," I said, my chin trembling. "Declan started it. He splashed me first, and then we got carried away."

"Do ya have any idea what time of year it is? You'll catch a cold." She shook her head and put her cigarette out in a green marble ashtray. "Come here ta me," she said, waving me over. She flung the tea towel from her shoulder and dabbed my face dry. A grin grew from one corner of her mouth as she winked at me, then flicked her chin toward the stairs. "Up wit' ya now. Get those clothes off before yer mum gets home. Go warm yourself in the bath. I'll collect yer clothes and get them washed and dried. Yer mum'll never know."

My eyes widened. "Really?"

"Go on already. Before I change me mind." Her exasperated scowl melted into a grin.

Her aged face bloomed like a soft rose when she smiled. Though her lips were lined and shrunken from smoking, and her teeth a nicotine yellow, her blue-green eyes still sparkled. The soft white curls that had escaped her low ponytail wrapped around her pearl earrings.

She swung her hand and smacked my bum. "Go!"

I bolted up the stairs.

There was a bump and light swerve, and my eyes shot open. I'd been dreaming.

Memories of Gran.

I swallowed down the rush of emotion, and then glanced around, disoriented, forgetting where I was. Rows of blue seats. An engine's whir hummed in my ears. A stranger's eyes stared at me from across my seat. I was on the bus to Carraig Brón.

I hugged my backpack closer, as it had almost fallen off my lap, and rubbed my eyes with the sleeve of my other arm. I peered out the window. It was night. We were not in a village or town—no lights.

I cracked the window, and the fresh scent of sea air hit my nose.

Home. We can't be far now.

I checked the time on my phone. I'd been on the bus for at least four hours. It was almost nine o'clock.

Gosh, I hope Pete's Pub is still open. It should be, given the Irish's late night manners. And, I'm starving. Irish pub food sounds amazing.

A sudden wave of anxiety hit my stomach. What if Don and Carla don't own the pub anymore? Sure, the village got tourists, but that was the only hotel in the whole town. Mostly only vacation homes in the carraig.

I rubbed my hand down my face.

What was I thinking?

Street lights shone in the distance, and then a green sign that said, "Carraig Brón 10km." My eyes widened, scanning for anything familiar. I leaned forward in my seat as we started passing homes on the outskirts of the village.

"Do ya mind closin' the window?" the stranger asked, a sharp glare flashing in his eyes.

"Right." I shut the window tight, stopping the cold air from coming in. "Sorry."

The stranger muttered something undecipherable under his breath.

I rolled my eyes. I wasn't about to let him rob me of this moment and stared back out the window. I could barely make out the cliff's edge cupping the shore.

Strange.

Where is the lighthouse? Do they even light it anymore?

The outline of the island wasn't visible either. It was too dark—clouds obscured the moon. I laughed to myself. I used to believe that Balor, the demon king of the giants, lived there.

I used to be so scared of his one eye finding me.

I chuckled again, then noticed the odd man still glaring at me.

What's his problem, anyway?

I tried smiling—maybe that would soften his glower. Nothing. He sat there, face rigid, unmoved by my act of civility.

Well, this is uncomfortable.

I shook my head.

I don't care. Let him glare.

The first lights shone from the carraig's small strip of shops. My heart beat faster. I stood and put my backpack on, holding onto the blue pole at the center of the aisle. My fingers itched to pull the cord and let the driver know this was my stop.

The village had a few shops like Nan's Boutique & Gifts, which carried postcards, souvenirs, and a pharmacy for tourists; Lem's post office; and a bookshop—duly named Book Shop. Pete's Pub & Inn, along with the local chipper, and Nicky's Take Away—the carraig's pizzeria—were the only restaurants.

At least that's how it was ten years ago.

A fancy-looking restaurant sat on the edge of the bay.

That's new!

"The Fisherman's Wharf," I whispered, reading the lit red-and-yellow sign decorated with an anchor emblem.

What else has changed?

My palms began to sweat. I glanced over my shoulder, as if an airplane waited behind me to take me back to Chicago. I didn't want to go back, but maybe Carraig Brón had changed too much over the years I'd been away. Maybe it was no longer home.

My nerves started to settle as we entered town through the lane of shops. Familiar signage and storefronts helped calm my nerves. I pulled the cord as the end of the street, where Pete's would be, came into view.

The bus slowed, pulling to the side. Two travelers seated outside the bus stop stood up as the bus screeched to a halt. I gripped the pole and stole one last look at the strange man who had finally stopped glaring at me. I grabbed my suitcase from the rack above, then fumbled through the narrow aisle toward the bus's open doors.

"Thanks," I said to the bus driver.

He grunted in reply, staring ahead. The typical Irish charm

was low on everyone's meter this evening. I shrugged and made my way off the bus. The new passengers shuffled past me and climbed aboard. The doors rolled shut, the squealy boost from the engine engaged, and the bus roared its way down the road.

I stood alone on the quiet street, the silence and solitude pressing in around me. No one was out. I lifted my gaze to Pete's. The red, old-world Celtic letters still spelled out the name Pete's Pub & Inn above the door. Blacked-out shades covered the windows, making it look as abandoned as I felt. Abandoned or not, I had no choice. This was the only option I had allowed for myself on this impulsive adventure.

The wheels on my suitcase rattled as they rolled over the sidewalk. A nervous lump crawled up my throat. Voices emanated from the other side of the sturdy wooden pub door.

"Thank God," I gasped, pushing the door open. The light and warmth of the interior hit my face. Beer, fish, and chips permeated the air. Patrons sat at tables inside the long narrow pub, eating and drinking.

At least I'll get something to eat tonight.

A young man wiped down the counter behind the bar. "Hullo!" he called with a small smile, not looking up from his work. I'd hoped Don would be behind the bar, greeting me with his broad smile, just like he did when Declan and I would come rambling in for some hot tea and chips after playing on the shore.

A tall, gum-smacking hostess appeared in front of me, making me jump. "Ya a'right, now?"

I laughed, grasping at my heart. "Sorry, I didn't see you."

She eyed my suitcase. "Em?"

"I just got into town. I haven't had a chance to offload anything yet."

"American?"

"Um? No, well, yes . . . I mean, sort of." My accent *had*

become less pronounced now that I'd been in the States for a decade.

She rolled her eyes. "Would ya like a table? Or just a seat at the bar?"

"Table please."

"Right." She grabbed a menu and motioned for me to follow.

My suitcase and I scrambled after her. "Can I ask—are Don and Carla here?"

She stopped walking, and I almost barreled into her. She turned, glaring at me, her dark eyeliner highlighting her striking blue eyes.

"I just, uh . . . I used to know them is all."

"What's yer name?"

"Nora. Nora Morrigan. I used to be a local. Hoped maybe they were here. Might like to see them."

"Hm? Sit here." She pointed to a table with two chairs.

I took off my backpack, settled myself into the offered chair, and took the menu she handed me. "Thanks."

"Yah, going ta' be eatin' anyt'ing?"

"Yes, please."

"Do ya know what ya want then? Or do ya need a minute?"

"Fish and chips, please . . . and . . . and some hot tea," I said, rubbing my sleeve over my cold nose. Autumn evenings were cold on the Irish coast.

"Right." The hostess spun on her heel and walked away.

"What is the deal?" I mumbled under my breath.

Is it just me or does everyone have an attitude problem?

Now that the hostess had gone, my stomach sank a little further into my toes. I situated my suitcase and backpack out of the way beneath the table. It didn't appear that Don was here anymore, and all hope that there might still be an inn for me to stay at was fading fast.

Should I even bother asking if there are rooms available?

I sighed, slumping in my chair.

Eat first.

I could problem-solve while I ate. I pulled my phone out of my pocket. I needed to start looking for a place to stay.

I think that was the last bus. Maybe I could get an uber to a hotel. Do they even have uber drivers out here?

I bit my lip. The battery on my phone was at five percent.

"Gggrrr!" My teeth ground together. "I can't believe this." I scanned the walls for an outlet. "Dang it—I need an adapter."

"Nora?"

The deep familiar voice jolted me. I turned around, and a much grayer version of Don stood outside the kitchen doors. His salt-and-pepper hair was cut short, just as it had always been, only now it matched a beard that wrapped his chin. His off-white jumper and ratty jeans were almost identical to the ones he'd worn when Declan and I were kids.

"Don!" I stood, unsure how to greet him. It had been so long.

"Well, look at ya. The very image of yer mum wit' those green eyes and dark curls."

The mention of Mom stung, but I distracted myself by pulling on the hairband around my wrist.

I'm sure all the travel has done a number on my curly hair— no wonder people have been giving me strange looks. I'm probably a frizzy disaster.

"I . . . I have been traveling all day," I said with a shy smile, running my fingers through my hair in a failed attempt to tame it. "I am sure I'm a mess." I took the hairband and knotted my hair on top of my head.

Hopefully, that's not worse.

"Goodness, gurl. What're ya doin' here?" He approached me with his hands out and placed them on my shoulders. "It is wonderful ta see a Flaherty here once again. Place hasn't been the same wit'out yer family."

I nodded, unsure what else to say.

"Ya must be hungry? Did ya order some food?"

I nodded again. "Fish and chips."

"Is that all? Come now. Ya must have some pudding." He turned his head and yelled over his shoulder. "Tracy. Bring this gurl some sticky toffee pud." He looked back at me. "And a cuppa?"

I smiled. "I already ordered some tea."

"Ah, wonderful." He motioned with his hand. "Sit. I'll join ya. Did ya only just get in?" he asked, pointing to my suitcase.

"Yeah."

Don sat across from me with an incredulous stare. "I never t'ought I would get the opportunity ta see ya or yer family again once we lost yer grandparents. How's yer mum and da?"

My chest tightened. "They're fine." I changed the subject. "I came here on my own. Kind of a last-minute decision. I just missed it so much. I wanted to see home again."

"Ya talked to Lem? Ya stayin' out at The Flaherty House?"

I shook my head. "I was hoping you had a room at the inn. I just got off the bus. I haven't even had the chance to see if my grandparents' house is open."

"Oh, now—we don't have the inn anymore. Myself and Carla are t'inking about selling Pete's, ta be honest wit' ya. The kids have all gone to the city now and are having babies. We want ta be closer ta the grandchildren."

"Oh," I said, my heart sinking a little.

What am I going to do?

"But don't worry. Carla and I still have the place upstairs— it's just not open ta the public anymore. I would be happy ta have ya stay. I just need ta straighten up a room for ya."

I sighed with relief. "Thank you so much. I hope I'm not imposing."

"Ah, now, happy ta have ya."

"Is Carla here?"

He shook his head. "She is visiting our oldest, Genie. She'll be back in a few days, now."

"I would love to see her." I dropped my gaze to the table. "That's sad you might be selling."

"Well, this place used ta run itself when Carraig Brón was smaller. Now we have a new pub wit' all the bells and whistles across the way. Micro-brews and some such. Nicer menu." He pointed at the door as though I could see through it. "Though the locals still like ol' Pete's best."

"I saw that new wharf restaurant."

"That and a kabob place." Don leaned back and crossed his arms. "It's just that Carla and I do not have the energy ta make this place what it should be. A small local pub is all we've ever been, but now we have ta be more. Plenty of buyers would make this place shine, if we just let it go." His eyes dipped to the table. "It is hard moving on from all that this village used ta be. But there is no going back, whether we stay or we go. Change comes, and it isn't a bad t'ing."

I couldn't have disagreed more. The idea of so much change twisted my insides. All I wanted was to come back to the "before" time. Before my life had been forever altered. Change felt like a curse.

I scratched my jaw. "Is it all different now?"

"Shush, no, my gurl. You'll see tomorrow. There is still plenty the same. A lot of the same people still millin' around. Most of the regular shops are still thrivin'."

That thawed my sadness, and a smile curled my lips.

"Comin' t'rough. Hot plate," Tracy interjected, as she navigated past the bartender at the kitchen door. She shook her head and rolled her eyes as if the bartender should've seen her coming. "Here ya go, then." She winked with a smile, setting my tea and milk in front of me, followed by the fish and chips. Her newfound warmth toward me added a pretty brightness to her face. "The pud will be out shortly."

Don grinned. "I t'ink you'll find those chips are the same."

I picked a hot fry from my plate and bit into it. The hot steam seared the roof of my mouth, and I huffed on the scalding piece of potato as it dropped onto my tongue. Once the fry cooled, I munched on it, grinning as the nostalgic flavor danced over my tastebuds.

"Flavored with salt, chile, paprika, garlic, and a little secret magic," Don said with a gleam in his eyes. "My own special blend."

"Same as always."

"Declan always likes extra seasoning."

"He did," I agreed, munching down another fry.

"Oh, he still does."

I stopped chewing. "Is Declan still here?"

3

The Haunts Return

"Thanks again," I said, wheeling my suitcase through the bedroom door.

Don stood in the doorway with an armload of clean, folded sheets and a towel. "Our kids come and stay wit' us often and use these rooms. They aren't too stale. Might just want ta fluff the duvet a bit. In the mornin', you should have a nice view of the sea."

I set my backpack on the floor before taking the linens from his arms.

He pointed down the hallway. "That first door on the left is the shower and washroom. Mine and Carla's space is at the other end, so ya have this whole corridor to yourself."

I squeezed the linens against my middle. "So nice to be back."

"Well, I cannot begin ta tell ya how happy it makes me ta see ya here. Carla will do a backflip when she hears. I will phone her in the mornin'. You'll be in the carraig for a few days, then?"

I nodded.

"Grand. She will want ta see ya." He patted the sides of his thighs as though all out of things to say. "Well, I'll leave ya now. G'night." He waved, then turned down the hallway.

"Good night," I called and shut the door. Relief washed

over me—I was home, and everything had fallen into place despite my moments of doubt. Seeing Don had warmed my heart, and I couldn't wait to see Carla. She had been a good friend to my mom.

Speaking of friends . . . learning that Declan often came to the village kindled a nervous hope that maybe I would see him too.

What if our friendship hadn't meant the same thing to him, though? What if he's forgotten about me?

My cheeks warmed. What was he like now? A lot could've changed in ten years. He was a year older than me—twenty-three.

Would I even recognize him? Would he recognize me?

I mostly looked the same. Just the twenty-two-year-old version of my twelve-year-old self. I walked over to the mirror. The dark circles under my eyes conveyed the type of day I'd had. Wild curls escaped from my messy top knot.

"Time for a shower," I said to myself, dragging my weary body toward the washroom. Exhaustion crept through my muscles, but the thought of washing off the stale smell of airplane and bus seats kept me moving—I couldn't sleep without a rinse.

I waited almost a full minute for the water to warm but only freezing droplets trickled into the tub. My hopes of a hot shower faded. I scrunched my brow and was about ready to retreat when I spotted the hot water cord.

I smacked my forehead, laughing.

Of course. I forgot the hot water cord. Irish plumbing.

I rolled my eyes and pulled the cord. The water heated immediately on my palm, and I stepped into the divine warmth, washing away all the stress of travel.

I squeezed the jasmine-and-bergamot-scented shampoo through my hair and charted my course for tomorrow.

I will go straight to Lem's and see if my grandparents' house is available.

If it was, maybe he would give me the keys right there. Eager butterflies flitted in my stomach.

Has the house changed?

The smell of Irish coastal water was different from the water in Chicago. I smiled as the stoney, mineral aroma wafted into my nose. Much better than the chlorinated Chicago water. The water cascaded over my skin like a hot, liquid blanket—just what I needed to escape, if only for a moment, from a whole world that had fallen apart, to pretend everything was back to how it was meant to be. Before Gran died. Before Dad ruined *everything*. Before Mom was also stolen away.

My breath caught in my chest. I quickly captured the swell of emotion and shoved it down.

Not here. Not tonight.

I turned off the water and grabbed my towel. The fresh, dry cotton against my face soothed the storm rising inside me.

"That's better," I said as I dried off and returned to my room, content that I would likely fall asleep quickly.

Pajamas on and bed made, I went to grab my phone from the nightstand. I needed to charge it.

"Ack! Forgot." The battery on my phone was in the red. "Can't charge it without an adapter." I sighed, blowing through my lips, and tossed my phone onto the clothes in my suitcase. "I'll have to buy an adapter tomorrow."

I switched off the lights and jumped into bed, perfectly burritoed in the lavender duvet. Sublime warmth filtered through me. I turned my head and peered at the window. The sheer curtains rippled as the wind drafted in from outside. The wind cried with a gentle, baleful moan, and I closed my eyes, allowing the sound to soothe me to sleep.

A lulling pitch broke through the tenor.

What is that?

I pulled the duvet closer to my chin. The mournful groan floated alongside the wind that sounded unnatural.

It's nothing.

I clamped my eyes shut, trying to ignore it, but the haunted cry persisted. The wind howled more fiercely.

It's just getting stormy.

I gulped that reassuring thought down.

Please let that be all it is.

The windows rattled, and the instinct to throw my covers over my head gnawed at my nerves. I squeezed my eyes tighter, ignoring my overwhelming fear.

I am not a child. Don't act so stupid—

A haunted voice emerged, crying louder than the wind—a voice almost . . . *human.*

It couldn't be.

I plugged my ears, and thoughts of my Gran's tales of the sluagh raced through my head.

"Don't let them call your name," Gran's voice reminded me.

"N-N-o-r-r-a!" A growling moan reverberated through the howling gale outside.

No. My mind is playing tricks on me.

"N-N-o-r-r-a!"

I shoved my fingers deeper into my ears. The windows rattled as if someone tried to break in. I gave in and thrust the blankets over my head.

I am not hearing it. I am not hearing anything. Just go to sleep.

But all the old fears I'd long forgotten returned all at once.

The windows banged louder, and louder.

This is stupid. I refuse to be afraid of the wind.

I tossed off the covers, sprang from my bed, and dashed toward the window. Teeth clenched, I gripped the latch and secured the French windows. My heart beat like a drum as I gazed out the glass. My eyes adjusted to the darkness, capturing the white-capped waves thrashing toward the shore. Grassy fronds between the white rocks flailed back and forth. Nothing more. No ghoulish phantom was out there calling my name.

"It's just a storm. See?" I said, trying to convince myself.

I placed my hand on my forehead and sighed, slowing my breaths.

A gleam of light captured my eye—the Toraigh Island lighthouse. Its lamp rotated around the sea line.

Have I already forgotten what it's like to live by the sea?

The windy timbre was all that remained. No more voices, or pervasive cries.

"I just need to go to sleep."

I closed the gap in the curtains and backtracked toward my bed. I wouldn't turn my back but instead glared at the window like it was still a threat. The duvet brushed my legs. I scooted back onto the mattress, lay down, and covered my head again.

The alarm bells still rang in my head, but exhaustion won the battle. I closed my eyes and fell asleep.

The crying of seagulls called me awake. My heart leapt.

That sound. I'm home.

Sunlight peeked through the sheer curtains. No remaining terrors from the night's storm.

Thank goodness.

I pulled the covers back and stretched. The room's icy coldness brushed my skin, and I quickly threw the covers back over me.

"Bbbrrr!" I trembled under the blankets. Goosebumps stippled my skin as the still-warm duvet enveloped me. I peered from my bed to the window. A brilliant blue sky peeked through the edge of the curtains. The seagulls' cackles filtered through my ears.

I always liked them. My grandad treated them like they

were just menaces that pooped on everything, but to me, their cawing always sounded like laughter.

I looked from the window to the wall heater.

"I wish I'd thought to turn *you* on last night."

I jumped from my bed and grabbed a sweater from my suitcase, and a pair of socks. I raced over to the heater, turned the dial to high, then leapt back into bed, waiting for it to warm up.

I am going to see Gran and Grandad's house today.

I smiled as I pulled my socks on underneath the covers, listening to the heater *tick, tick, tick* as it warmed. It's probably not even that cold of a day, but these old Irish buildings never held their heat well. They were like refrigerator boxes, even on milder autumn days.

Much colder in Chicago. But at least there we have central heating.

I wrapped the duvet around myself and shuffled to the window. The carraig was a friendlier scene now that the sun was out. People meandered the shore with their dogs. A small bustle of people sauntered along the main street. I leaned forward, peering farther down the lane. The green colors of Lem's post and shop barely peeked out from the building in front of it. *Oifg an Phoist, Carraig Brón* was written on the hanging sign attached to the top side of the small adjoining building, just past his bookshop.

I wonder if Declan is there.

He was Lem's son.

I sighed, holding my hand over the heater that now put off a good deal of heat. I waddled over to my suitcase and picked out a black hoodie and a pair of jeans, then brought them over to the heater to change next to the warmth.

My cheeks were pink by the time I made it over to the mirror to do my hair and makeup.

I look more rested.

I rubbed the remnants of black eyeliner from beneath my eyes. My curls were in full form, as if happy to be back by the sea.

Going to have to tame you.

I pointed my hairbrush at my shoulder length hair in the mirror.

I think it would be best to tie you back up.

A little blush, some mascara, and a satisfactory knot on top of my head with cascading curls was the best I could do. I tamed the ringlets of fringe that hung around my face, twisting the tendrils between my fingers, then put on my blue running shoes. I grabbed my backpack, jacket, and phone, and headed down the stairs.

"Awe, look at ya now," Don said from behind the bar, as I entered the main pub. "Much brighter now after havin' some proper sleep. Were ya comfortable enough?"

I smiled and nodded. "The room was perfect."

The pub was quiet, and sunlight poured through the windows, brightening the space. A few patrons sipped tea at the back-end booths. I peeked through the windows at the hustle and bustle of the street.

"Seems ya brought a storm wit' ya last night."

"I know," I huffed, joining him on a barstool. "The wind was howling. I forgot how loud it gets here on the shore."

"Did it keep ya awake?"

I shook my head. "Slept fine," I lied.

"Can I get ya some tea? We have a full Irish breakfast if yer hungry. Afraid that's all at this hour."

"Some tea would be nice."

Don turned and poured hot water from a kettle into a teapot. "Talked ta Carla this mornin'. She can hardly wait ta see ya. Almost considered coming home early, but then I convinced her ya wouldn't be leavin' too quickly. That was right, now?" he asked, turning back around with a white teapot and mug in his hands. He set them on the counter in front of me.

"I will be here."

He beamed with a wide smile. "Milk? Sugar?"

"Yes, please."

He fetched me the accouterments. "How long will ya be stayin'?"

"Honestly?" My brows pinched as I poured some tea into my mug, then added the milk. The reddish-brown and white swirled together, making me wish it had answers for me. "I haven't really decided—I sort of bought a one-way ticket."

Don's head turned, and he leaned toward me.

I didn't look up. "I'm not feeling anxious to leave. It'll probably depend on if Gran and Grandad's house is available."

"Sure Lem will make it so."

"Well, I wouldn't want to put anyone out that had it reserved."

"Ya know ya also have a room here as long as ya need one." Don's eyes stayed on me for a long moment. I shifted in my chair and glanced up. His stare had turned more serious. "Now, gurl, it may not be any of my business, but is everyt'ing all right wit' ya?"

No. Not right now. I want to pretend. At least for a while longer.

"Mmhm." I bit my lip, avoiding his eyes. "I just really missed home. And I have time right now."

But do I? Should I really just ignore the classes at the expensive school my dad pays for?

I took a big swig of my hot tea. It burnt my throat, and I coughed.

"Are ya a'right?"

I held up my hand as I hacked until tears burned my eyes. "O—kay," I managed to squeeze from my throat. "App—parently . . . *cough* . . . I prefer to inhale my tea."

Don chuckled and got me a glass of water. "Here ya' go. That'll help."

I chugged the water, then cleared my throat. "Do you mind if I leave my things in the room for now? I'm anxious to see if Lem is at the post office. Plus, I need to buy an adapter for my phone. Forgot to do that before my trip."

Don's eyes danced over my face, then narrowed as if working to uncover what was hidden behind them. He sighed with a smile. "Of course, gurl—yer t'ings aren't botherin' anyone where they are." He pointed toward the door. "There might be adapters in the shop next to Lem's. If not, ya might have ta go up the road to the Tesco grocery shop. I could give ya a lift later if ya need one. Also, Lem has a new little coffee addition ta their bookshop over there. Might even have some nice sausage rolls."

That put a smile on my face. Sausage rolls did sound delicious. I missed eating them. "Thanks," I said, getting up from the stool. "Don—I am happy to pay for the room last night. And certainly for the tea and the food."

"No, gurl." He waved his hands and shook his head. "Just like old times, yer money's never been any good here."

"You sure?"

Don frowned. "Come on now. Yer about ta hurt my feelings."

"Okay, then—thanks," I said with a grin. "Well, I'm going to head over to Lem's. I'll let you know how it goes. Tell Carla I can't wait to see her."

"She will want ta know all about yer mum. She misses her somethin' fierce. She was one of her best mates and hasn't gotten ta catch up wit' her in a while. Maybe she will give yer mum a call."

The knives drove into my heart, stinging my already fragile defenses.

Just pretend.

My voice barely broke the silence, as though a single word might break the dam. "Right. Tha—that would be nice. My mom"—I swallowed hard—"she's not home right now. I'll . . . I'll let Carla know when she's back. She can call her then."

Don's eyes searched mine, and something shifted in his expression. His brows knitted.

That look. He can see it, can't he?

The tears—they pressed into my eyes.

Get out! Quick.

I turned toward the door and ran out into the cool air, leaving Don behind.

4

Coffee & Post

Just like I thought.

It wasn't that cold out. The wind barely cooled my tears as I wiped them away and strode down the sidewalk. I didn't dare turn around just in case Don had come outside to check on me. I quickened my pace, half-jogging to the post office. I slowed just before reaching the door and drew deep breaths to steady myself.

Remember where you are. You're home. It's better. Things will be better.

I puffed through my lips one more time and moved toward the door. But one door down, a pink building captured my attention. It was located right where Lem's bookshop used to be, with "Della's" written on the large shop window.

"Della?" I said with a smile. That was Declan's little sister's name. I passed the post office and went inside.

The warm, sweet smell of cinnamon flooded my senses. A small coffee bar stood along the right-side wall, connected by an open entryway to the post office. Instead of a bookshop, it was now a café, with a gift shop to boot. Small, Victorian-style tables lined the front windows, adorned with fresh flowers and intricate lace runners. A few bookshelves remained against the back walls. The space exuded warmth and elegance, chasing away my sorrows, leaving me grateful to have stepped inside.

"Hello," said a tall, full-figured girl from behind the coffee bar. She tinkered with the espresso machine, then turned in my direction. Her round rosy cheeks and richly lashed brown eyes were instantly recognizable. Della. I hadn't seen her since she was little. She couldn't have been more than nineteen. Her youthfulness was still displayed in her two braided, auburn pigtails and vibrant clothes.

"Hi," I said back.

"Welcome to Della's. Can I get ya a coffee?"

Her sweet, sing-songy voice made me smile. "Um, yah," I said, walking over to the counter. "Lovely café."

"Oh, t'anks." She grinned. "It's mine. I'm Della."

I nodded and looked over the café menu. She hadn't recognized me. Of course, we didn't ever play together as kids. She was just there sometimes, in the background, playing with her dollies, when Declan and I would tumble past.

The menu was as pink as the exterior. Purple detailed the border with a sort of fancy, delicatessen vibe.

"My da and I just recently opened this café," Della said, as I perused the menu. "It was an old bookshop before. Didn't really bring a load of tourists, and I've been beggin' my da to let me run my own café. Not a ton o' those around here."

"That's true," I said, noticing the sparkle in her eyes as she spoke about the café. "I remember the bookshop."

"You've been around before?"

"Yeah, um—" I hesitated, wrestling with a surge of nerves. *Do I tell her who I am?*

"I, uh—I used to live here, but I've been gone for a while."

"No way." She leaned forward, eyes narrowing as she searched my face.

"I was still a kid when—"

"Eh?" A man popped his head around the post office entryway. His eyes locked onto me. "Oh, my dear merciful Mary!" He gaped as he stumbled through the opening.

He looked exactly the same. His hair was buzzed short, fading into his balding crown. Dark whiskers created a five-o'clock shadow that never went away. He always had the roundest, kindest brown eyes.

"Hi, Lem. Remember me?"

"Nora Morrigan—what're ya doin' here, child?" He cupped his hand over his mouth. "Look at ya?" He walked around the corner of the coffee bar toward me. "You're all grown up, just like Declan and my Della." He whistled through his lips, gazing past me. "Has yer mum come wit' ya?"

"No—it's just me."

The corners of his mouth dropped with clear disappointment. He and my mom had been friends since childhood. Just like me and Declan. His eyes centered back on mine. "Well now, what're ya doing here? Absolutely stunned ta see ya."

"Who is this, Da?" Della asked.

"Ya know—the Morrigans?"

She grimaced, as though trying to remember.

"They own the old Flaherty House down the road."

Her eyes widened. "Oh yah!" She put her hands on her hips with a teasing smirk. "Declan's girlfriend. The one that broke his heart by leavin' him years back."

Heat rose to my face. "What?"

"Della!" Lem tsked, shaking his head. "What's wrong wit' ya?" He glanced back at me. "She's just tryin' ta stir up trouble." Lem grabbed my shoulders and pulled me into a hug. He patted me on the back, then pulled away to take another look at me. "Gosh, gurl, it's great ta see ya! So much like yer—"

"Hey, Da!" called a deep voice through the back door. In lumbered someone holding a tower of boxes.

My breath caught in my chest, and I fought the urge to dash out the front door.

"The supply man just delivered a giant load of these envelopes for the shop." He hefted the heavy boxes onto the counter, then stepped out from behind them. "He said that he left some samples for ya ta—"

His eyes noticed mine, and he stopped.

More heat flooded my cheeks. His lash-lined green eyes and chiseled chin were not what I had expected. Someone had taught him how to tame his short, thick, brown hair. When we were younger, his hair always fell into his eyes, but now it was nicely styled, swooping back from his forehead. And he was tall. So tall. I looked down at the floor.

"Declan," Lem said, presenting me with his hand. "You remember Nora."

I dared to peek up at him, feigning confidence with a small smile.

He seemed awestruck as he stared at me. His brows pressed tight and he lowered his eyes. When he glanced back up, one corner of his mouth lifted as he leaned against the counter. "She's come back."

Della leaned onto her elbows and winked. "Isn't she the one who used ta knock down all those rock towers that took ya hours ta build?"

"The very one," he said, with an ever-growing smile. The spark in his grin revealed the boy I used to know.

"I, uh . . ." I mumbled, tugging on a curl beside my ear. "I'm sorry about that. Don't do that sort of thing anymore."

"So, now tell me," Lem said, breaking the awkward tension. "How long are ya here for?"

"Um . . ." I turned to Lem, folding my nervous hands together in front of me. "That's kind of why I came to see you. I—I wanted to see if the house was open. I . . . I wanted to stay for a while."

Lem's eyes flared. "Ya want ta stay?"

"Well"—I quickly collected my story—"I am on break from school, and I just really wanted to come home."

Declan's smile broadened at my remark.

"Why didn't yer da call me about this? I could've had the place better prepared for ya."

"I kind of made this decision without my dad's permission." I winced, hoping that Lem might give me an understanding nod. Instead, he just raised his brow. "It's not as though I'm a child. I don't need my dad's permission for this."

"Except that The Flaherty House is in his and yer mum's name—not yers, missy. They'll be missing out on the rental money while yer here. That is unless ya plan on payin' the fees."

My face fell. I didn't have the money to rent the house myself.

"Hey, now . . ." Lem said, cupping my chin and lifting my face. "I don't know what's goin' on wit' ya, but I'm not going ta be the one holdin' ya back from it. I know I'm not the only one who's happy that yer here." He winked at Declan, then sighed. "Besides, the place has been vacant for a couple months now, and it isn't as though we are headed into tourist season. Yer father's going ta have ta keep payin' the bills for that house, renters or no. I'll let ya explain yerself to yer da. I won't be gettin' involved."

"Thanks, Lem."

"Course. Now, I need ta go get ya the keys and tell Patty you've come so she can get a roast going. There's no way we won't be havin' ya over for supper. That's not up for debate." He disappeared into the post office and returned jingling two keys on a keyring. "Declan, yer around for the day, aren't ya? Why don't ya take Nora up ta the house and help her get settled in."

"Happy ta," he said with a shyish-looking grin, grabbing the keys from Lem.

"I need to buy an adapter for my phone charger," I blurted.

"Mmm," Lem mumbled. "You'll need ta go ta Tesco for tha'."

"I have ta run up ta town and get those few t'ings ya need

for the shop, anyway," Declan said. "I'll take her. Let me get my jacket." He ducked out of the café into the post office.

"I want ta come," Della hollered after him.

"No!" Declan shouted from the other end of the shop.

"Da," she whined, tilting her head, lips pursed and arms crossed.

I held in a giggle.

I remember her whining like that when she was little.

"Della, this is what I'm talkin' about. Ya can't run a shop, and then just leave. Ya have responsibilities."

"But I want ta talk ta Nora. She's gotta be properly loaded with memories Declan's kept from me. Please, Da."

Lem shot his hands out like a ref calling timeout. "No, Della, ya can't just leave work when ya feel like it. You can dish wit' her during supper."

Della gave me a mischievous grin. "Lucky ya didn't have me chattin' when yous were twelve."

A bell signaling a customer entering the post office caught Lem's attention. "Got ta go." He squeezed my arm. "We'll see ya at supper. I'll ring Declan wit' the details once I have 'em." He stepped into the post office. "Right, how are ya, Marta!"

"Jus' fin, jus' fine," muffled back the customer.

The banter with Lem and his customer went on, and suddenly Della had me by the arm, dragging me over to the coffee bar. "So, what can ya tell me about you and Declan?" She winked as she tamped some coffee grounds into the espresso portafilter. She twisted it into the machine and clicked the button. Soon, golden-brown liquid drained down the silver spouts into the two small glasses below. She filled a pitcher with milk, then glanced at me while she steamed it. "So?"

I laughed at her persistence. "Honestly, I am not sure what all I could tell you. I haven't seen him for years. I just hoped he'd remember me."

That sounded eager. Why did I say that?

"Hoped, eh?" She giggled, pouring the espresso into a cup, then formed a leaf pattern with the frothed milk. She scooted the cup toward me and handed me a lid.

I took a sip of the creamy liquid. "Mmm, very nice."

"I've got the talent. Still convincin' my da, though. I like baking as well." She pointed at a small pastry case on the other side of the bar's countertop. Some scones and muffins filled the case. "You want one? Sold out of the sausage rolls earlier. Don't make those, though."

My shoulders slumped. I'd wanted one. "Sure." I shrugged.

"Blueberry's the best."

"Okay, I'll take one."

She took a small pastry bag, loaded a muffin inside, and handed it to me.

"Thanks." I got my card out to pay her.

"Nah." She waved her hand. "Next time ya come. So, what's the story? Ya know Declan used ta never stop talkin' about ya. He was always goin' on—"

Declan appeared around the corner and smacked Della's arm. "Lies!"

"Oh, hi, Declan," she chortled, rolling her eyes.

"Della likes ta flap her lips." He shoved Della, then, barely meeting my eyes, steered me toward the door. "Come on, let's go."

I slapped the lid on my drink and grabbed the muffin. "Thanks again for the coffee." I shuffled after Declan who led the way out the door.

"You can't keep her from me," Della sang after Declan. "Bye, Nora. See yous later."

Once we were out on the sidewalk, he shoved his hands in his pockets. "The car's just up here." He motioned with his shoulder and chin.

"Okay."

"My"—he worked his jaw—"my sister just says t'ings. She likes ta make me uncomfortable."

I noticed.

"I can't believe how different she is from the last time I saw her. She used to be so small."

He peered sideways at me. "Well, it's been a long time."

"Ten years."

His brows lifted. "Yah—I know."

"Have I changed?"

"I don't know. Haven't spent enough time wit' ya yet."

I chuckled. "I mean—do I look different?"

He seemed hesitant to respond. "Em—I guess. You're older, but ya still look like you."

That response warmed my heart. "Well, that's good, I guess."

A weird pressure built inside me to tell him I was sorry. The reason why escaped me. It wasn't as though I had done something wrong. It hadn't been *my* choice to leave. But, I couldn't help feeling guilty anyways—toward all of them.

I looked down at my feet. "You know, I never wanted to leave."

"I know."

"Ever since, I've just wanted to come back."

"What brought ya back now?"

"Funny thing," I said, a surge of honesty welling up inside me. "I was at the airport. I was supposed to fly back to school in Oregon from Chicago. But instead, I used my dad's credit card to buy a one-way ticket here."

He gasped. "You what?"

"Don't tell your dad."

"When did ya get here?"

"Last night."

His mouth fell open. "What? Where did ya stay?"

"At Don's inn. He let me stay in one of the old rooms."

He laughed, running his hand down his face. "That sounds like you."

"It does?"

"Yes—you've always been the mischievous sort."

"I have?"

I never really thought of myself as mischievous.

"Oh, come on now. You were always runnin' off down ta the shore when yer mum was looking for ya. Stealing yer Gran's bakes so you and I could eat them down in our clubhouse in the rocks."

"You remember that?" I beamed.

"Course I do. Lucky we got ta play together; you were always gettin' in trouble wit' yer da. I was always worried they might try ta separate us. You remember that time ya snuck one of yer gran's cigarettes?"

I gasped. "Oh, my God. I completely forgot about that. That didn't turn out so well."

He chuckled. "We both started vomiting in the sand."

"Haven't touched one of those death sticks since." I snorted.

We both cracked up, laughing even harder.

"Me either." Declan's eyes watered from laughing. "I remember how green ya turned. Thought we were both going ta have ta go to the hospital. Then after we puked, we had ta go wash off in the ocean. You got in so much trouble for gettin' yer uniform wet."

"I was always in trouble for getting my uniform wet."

Declan was the same as I remembered him. All the memories flooded back in like beautiful shells upon the shoreline. Being near him lightened the weight I carried in my heart. The home I hoped to find in Carraig Brón was more tangible in his presence, its essence alive in the warmth of Declan's laughter. "Glad I did it, though."

"What, stole yer gran's cigarette?"

I smiled, shaking my head. "No. I am glad I bought that ticket."

"What's going ta happen when yer da finds out?"

"I don't know. Honestly, not sure I care." A swirl of anger pulsed through my veins. "I only know I'm not going to let him take me away again. He can't. I'm not a child. I'll leave when I want to leave. Don't really care if I *ever* see him again, anyway."

Declan slowed his traipse, then stopped and looked at me. "Ya a'right, Nora?"

"I don't know," I mumbled before daring to meet his eyes. He looked at me like Don had—like Lem had. Was it really that apparent that something was wrong?

Just pretend.

"I'm—"

I found it harder to pretend around Declan. He was always like that—someone I could tell all my secrets to. Now that I was with him, that pull was there again.

I could tell him what happened. No. No, I'm not ready.

"My spontaneity has unsettled me a little. You know how it is. Big risk. And like you said, I know my dad isn't going to be happy when he finds out. Maybe he won't for a while."

"Maybe," Declan said, biting his bottom lip.

"I'm fine. Really."

"Ah well, tis just good ta see ya, anyway." He started walking again, and I breathed a sigh of relief. "Car's over there." He pointed to a blue Hyundai.

"Is that your car?"

"Yah." He grinned. "Ya like her?"

"Her, huh?"

"Course." He laughed. "She's great at getting me back and forth from school and the carraig."

"You still live here?"

"No. Go to uni in Donégal. But it's not far. I come home ta

help Da out. Gets me some extra euros ta buy petrol for taking rebellious gurls ta Tesco."

I laughed, feigning a shocked gasp. "I'm not rebellious."

Not usually.

"Ya know ya are." He winked. "Now get in the car." He clicked his key fob, and the doors unlocked.

I reached for the door.

Declan was beside me, lifting one brow. "Are ya drivin'?"

"Oh." I peered in through the window. The steering wheel was on the wrong side of the car. "Right." I shook my head and giggled my way around to the passenger seat on the left-hand side of the car.

"Not in Chicago anymore, are ya?"

"Thank God for that."

5

Landan

Nervous excitement coursed through me as we pulled up to The Flaherty House.

Wow! It hasn't changed a bit.

At least not on the outside. Same white-washed clay exterior and thatched roof. My heart raced and my body tensed. My eyes moistened as I clicked open the car door and stepped outside.

I've been waiting ten years to see this house again.

"Ya want ta see inside first?" Declan asked. "We can come back and get the rabbit food ya bought back there."

"Rabbit food?" I gasped with feigned shock. "Don't judge me for eating healthy."

He chuckled and strode toward the door, pulling the keys from his pocket.

I would be staying for an undetermined amount of time, so I picked up some groceries while we got the adapter at Tesco.

I rolled my eyes at him, then turned, glimpsing the sea. My grandparents' house sat on a plateau, perched above a low cliff-face by the shore.

I scrambled to join Declan, but movement from above caught my eye. I paused.

Declan seemed to notice. "What is it?"

I pointed to my old bedroom window. It was wide open, and the sheer curtains of my childhood swirled in the wind.

Declan joined me and peered up. "That's strange. My da was just here the other day. He makes sure everyt'ing is buttoned up tight."

"Hm?" I shrugged. "Probably just a loose latch. It was really windy last night." Fright surged through my veins at the memory.

Don't think about it. The wind did not call my name. I just imagined it. I was tired.

"Well, we'll make sure ta shut it up now, anyway."

I nodded and followed him to the door. Something brushed my leg.

"Aaahh!" I screamed, jumping against Declan and squeezing his arm.

"What in the world?" he yelled, stumbling backward against the house beside the front door.

I grasped at my chest and looked down. A green-eyed, black cat meowed at me from the front step.

Declan laid his hands on my shoulders. "Steady now, it's just Buttons."

"Buttons?"

"Yah." He crouched and gave the cat's chin a scratch. "Sorry if Nora frightened ya. They apparently don't have cats in Chicago."

"They do so." I shoved Declan. "I just didn't see *him*." I glanced down at the cat. It blinked its eyes and meowed again. I knelt and petted the cat as it rubbed its silken cheek against my knee.

"He hangs out around here. We feed him sometimes. There's some food in the house for him." He smiled at the cat. "I'll get ya some food, Buttons. If I can only get this door open without any more drama"—Delcan shot me a sarcastic look—"then we'll *all* be a little better off."

I put my hands on my hips and smirked. "No one's holding you back."

He chuckled, put the key in the door, and clicked it open. The stale smell of Gran's cigarettes didn't whack me in the face. Instead, I took in the sweet fragrance of vanilla air fresheners. My heart sank more as Declan turned on the lights. The walls were painted white, and the old brown and tan carpet was gone—replaced with laminate wood flooring.

My eyes raced to find any sign of familiarity. "It's different."

"Yer da had us hire some remodelers some years ago. We needed ta get rid of the smoke smell." He scrunched his nose and pointed around the house. "So, carpet had ta go, and the walls needed ta be treated and painted. My da made sure ta hold onto some of the old furniture that was still good. Me ma decorated wit' some newer additions too." He motioned toward my grandparents' mid-century, green vinyl sofa. My beating heart calmed as I spotted it beside my gran's coffee table and lamp—though the shade was different. My gran's art deco peacocks still hung on the wall—I'd always liked looking at them.

"My ma really liked some of yer gran's retro t'ings. Anyt'ing still in good shape, she tried ta use."

"Probably wasn't a lot of it." I dragged my shoe across the gray faux wood, missing the ugly brown carpet that once covered it.

He shook his head. "Not down here."

I drifted toward the kitchen, my emotions a mixed bag. I wanted it to be the same.

Gran, my mom . . . even the bookstore. Time stole it all away. Why does everything have to change?

But, of course, it wouldn't be the same. What was I expecting? It'd been made into a hollow vacation home. My grandparents didn't live here.

Not sure this is home. Not anymore.

The yellow dining table was the same, but the chairs had been switched out. A new silver light fixture hung above it with a cone of white-frosted glass. The cupboards had also been painted white, which brightened the space. Granite countertops were complete with new stainless-steel appliances.

I bit my cheeks to stay calm.

Declan stood back, as though careful to give me some space.

How is it, after all these years, he still knows how to read me?

I opened the cupboard to the left of the sink, and a tear slid down my cheek. I reached for Gran's coffee mug. My chin trembled. It was the white one with the ugly green, yellow, and orange mushrooms. I wanted to kiss it. I held a piece of my gran—a piece of my old life in my palm.

Things were so much easier then.

"Made sure my ma kept that one." Declan's cheeks reddened, and he cast his gaze to the floor. "Ya used ta mention it all the time. I t'ought ya might be sad if it was gone."

He knew I'd come back one day. Or at least he'd hoped.

I nodded, still staring at the cup with tears floating in my eyes. I sniffled and looked up at Declan. "Would you like some tea?"

His eyes locked on mine, then he smiled. "Let me go get the rabbit food"—he winked—"from the boot of the car."

We enjoyed some tea. Delcan still drank his with a heavy dose of sugar. I grinned on the inside.

Some things haven't changed.

"Gotta go back ta the shop ta help my da. I'll be back in"—he glanced at his watch, then pressed his lips together—"a few hours or so." He set his mug on the table, stood, and grabbed his jacket.

My heart sank. I didn't want to be alone. "See you later, then?"

"Yah." He nodded, smiling as he walked out the door. He cast me one last look before he closed the door.

"Bye," I whispered to no one there.

I sat on the vinyl couch, Gran's empty tea mug still in my hands and peered toward the door that led to the downstairs bedrooms and stairway. That part of the house created a chasm in my chest.

How much has it changed?

The key that unlocked the door to the stairs lay in front of me on the coffee table. Declan had said they put a lot of the boxed-up items my mother wasn't ready to get rid of in the bedrooms upstairs. Vacationers weren't allowed up there—thus the lock.

I laid my head on the sofa. A faint cigarette smell wafted into my nose. I didn't like the smell of cigarettes, but in this house, it was the essence that Gran had been here. Without it, it was like she was never here. I had a harder time imagining her and Mom at the dining room table. That was where I found them most evenings. My grandad liked to stand by the front window and stare out at the sea with his hands on his hips. My dad was almost always away on business. That's why we lived with my grandparents.

"I need to get out of here." I stood and set the mug on the table. I'd wanted to come home, but now—

It's all gone.

I pressed my lips together. Anger at what my dad had stolen from me blasted through my veins.

SLAM!

A loud noise crashed from upstairs—the wind howled.

I clutched my chest.

Probably just the upstairs window.

I gulped the adrenaline down, then raced for my jacket. I was out the door in a flash, staring up at the windows. Sure enough, they banged back and forth from the wind gusts.

Meow.

Button's large, round eyes peer up at me.

"Declan already fed you," I said, choosing to ignore him. There was a divot at the edge of the plateau, where a path led down to the shore. I glanced back at the cat. "I am going on a walk."

Buttons blinked at me in response.

"You have to stay here."

I moved toward the trail. Buttons followed at my heels.

"You can't come. The shore is not a good place for a kitty."

I picked up my pace so the cat would get the hint. The trailhead was before me, and I leapt down onto the rocky path. I glanced over my shoulder. The cat remained on the ledge above.

Ha! Try to follow me now.

I pointed to the cat with my index finger. "Stay." I strode down the trail—the same trail I took every day to meet Declan when I was a kid. The grassy stones looked the same as I traipsed over them. I peered back. The cat sat at the top of the trailhead staring down at me.

Good. Last thing I need is to be bothered by a cat.

I set my eyes on the shore. The mix of pebbles and sand would soon be beneath my feet. The temperature continued to drop the closer I got to the beach. I shoved my hands into my jacket pockets, wishing my windbreaker had a fleece lining.

I used to have no trouble with the cold. Nothing held me and Declan back from getting wet every time we went to the shore. Now, I wouldn't want the icy waters chilling my dry clothes.

The flat rocks became more like steep stairs, and I slowed my pace so I didn't trip. I jumped off the final stone, and my feet hit the firm, wet sand. The wind picked up, but the waves were not too wild. They gently brushed the shore while the seagulls pecked the pebbles for morsels.

The sun in the cloudless sky warmed my skin despite the cold breeze. I closed my eyes and let the sunlight rest on my cheeks, then stole a deep breath of the clean sea air.

My mind drifted away from the torrent of pain. I didn't want to miss my mom right now. I didn't want to miss my gran. I just wanted to find home.

I wish I could just forget it all.

I opened my eyes. Not far up the beach was a large driftwood tree that lay on its side. Perfect place to sit and watch the sea. I walked over and crawled onto a bench-like nook in what used to be a gnarled root. I pulled my knees close, tucked my arms between my legs and torso, and gazed at the gray waves. The lighthouse at Toraigh Island jutted above the sea like a lonely stone giant. The red and white colors from the beacon's tower seemed lonelier than me—which brought me a little comfort.

I glanced back up the hill. The cat wasn't there anymore.

Good.

I closed my eyes again, letting the rhythm of the waves wash over me. The gentle rush of the water silenced my thoughts. The echo of Declan's laughter mingled with mine.

A chill ran down my spine, and I pulled my legs in tighter. A shadow passed in front of my vision. A cloud perhaps? I kept my eyes closed.

"Hi, Nora!"

My eyes shot open. A tall man, silhouetted by the sun, stood in front of me. I yelped and jumped back against the wood, bumping my head.

"Ow," I groaned, rubbing the back of my head.

The man stepped closer, the sunlight lifting the shadow from his face.

I hissed through my teeth, "Sorry, do I know you?"

He stood there with a smile.

Wait . . . those eyes . . . that grin.

He'd changed more than Declan had. He'd been such a small, thin-faced boy when we'd played together.

If that's what you'd even call what we did.

Every now and again, when Declan was off building his towers, we'd sit and talk until it was time to go home. But now he was tall—maybe six foot or more. His shoulders were even broader than Declan's. His dark, raven hair blew about his face. His bangs tousled over his deep green eyes. He wore a black pea coat, his hands deep inside the pockets.

"Landan?" I said, with a surprised gape. "Gosh. Look at you. You still living in the carraig?"

"Ah, yah. This is my home. Heard ya'd come back. Thought maybe I would find ya at the shore."

I continued to rub the ache at the back of my head.

"Sorry I startled ya."

"Yeah, you really snuck up on me."

"Tried not ta, but ya had yer eyes closed." He came over and joined me on the log. His black lashes curled out from underneath his hooded eyes. His cheeks were ruddy from the wind.

"Declan was here earlier. Do you see much of him when he's in town?"

He shook his head.

The instant familiarity wasn't there with Landan like it was with Declan. He seemed more reserved, not as open and bright as Declan. And, I couldn't quite remember what he used to be like.

He sat there and stared at the sea. "It's good you've come back, Nora."

"Really. Why?"

He shrugged, then met my gaze. My heart skipped a beat at the brightness of his eyes, and the whites of his teeth beneath his smile. My face heated, and I fixated on the beach pebbles.

"It's been a little darker around the carraig since the Flahertys all left. Left a hole that sucked hope right out of the town."

That was a weird thing to say, but then . . . now I'm curious.

I leaned in. "How?"

"Don't ya know? Haven't ya noticed?"

I shook my head. "Noticed what?"

"How the folks are? Why do ya t'ink that is?"

I pressed my brows together. "I don't know. Why would that have anything to do with me?"

His brow furrowed. "It's just good yer back."

My family can't have mattered that much.

But then, I'd longed for the carraig every day for ten years. I left Declan. Mom left Carla and Lem. Everything felt wrong after my dad made us leave.

Still does.

"I want to stay," I said. Sadness tugged on my heart.

"Why can't ya?"

"I—"

"Don't ya get ta make that decision for yerself?"

Yes. But also no.

"I just haven't had a chance to figure things out yet. It was a spontaneous decision to come back."

"Needed ta come home?"

I narrowed my eyes. "Yeah—something like that." My nerves tensed, and I folded my arms. Landan presumed a lot for someone I hadn't spoken to in a long time. He wasn't like Declan. I stood to my feet and peered toward the house. "Nothing is quite the same as it used to be."

"That's a'right, isn't it?"

"I'm not so sure."

"I never got ta tell ya that I am sorry ya lost yer gran."

No.

His words pressed on the wall I tried to hide behind.

Let me pretend.

I nodded. "Thanks. It was a long time ago."

He took a deep breath. "Well, it's been a long time wit'out closure. That can feel like an everlasting curse."

"Huh," I murmured, struggling for a response. His words struck something deep within my spirit, like an iron prod stoking embers in a fire. I loved and loathed the sensation all at once. It was as if he held a truth I couldn't grasp—a truth that both pulled me closer and made me want to flee.

He followed my gaze up the hill. "Ya want me ta walk ya home?"

"Sure."

"Grand." He stood to his feet. "Come on." He led the way forward, and I scrambled to walk alongside him. At the first rock step, he held out his hand.

"I can do it." I blushed.

"I know," he replied, with an electric grin that sent butterflies through my belly, "but ya don't always have ta do it all by yerself."

A gasp caught in my chest. Tears threatened. When have I ever not had to do it by myself?

Never. I've been alone ever since Gran died. Is that what my dad wanted—to rip me away from everyone I loved? It sure seemed like it.

I twisted my lips and let my hand fall into Landan's waiting palm.

"There ya go," he said, assisting me all the way up until the rocks turned into a flat inclining trail again.

We walked up the hill in silence.

Nice to be around someone that doesn't need to fill the void with words. I like that.

"Here we are," he said, giving me a hand to the top.

"Thanks, Landan."

He nodded with *that* "you-need-to-know-your-important-and-I'm-telling-you-so" grin. He peered over at the house, and his face shifted. His brows lowered and his lips tightened. I wasn't sure what the look meant, but it gave me goosebumps. He pointed at the open window. "Ya need ta shut that." His eyes centered on mine. "And keep it shut."

"Uh, what?" I took a nervous step back.

"There are t'ings. T'ings ya don't understand. Anyway—you'll be safe enough now."

Now?

Fear drove its nails into my gut. "Landan, please don't tell me you buy into all that superstitious crap," I teased. I was desperate for his face to soften and tell me he'd been joking.

"Yer going to Declan's family's house tonight?" His eyes scanned the house, then met mine. The warning remained.

"Yes."

"Grand." His face softened, seeming pleased.

I crossed my arms. "Wait, how did you know that?"

He began to walk away, then stopped. "Be sure ta shut the window before ya leave."

"Landan?"

He hollered over his shoulder, "Jus' know that I'm here if ya need any help."

"Why would I need help?" I shouted after him, but he just waved without looking back and continued down the road.

"That was creepy." I shook my head as he disappeared around the corner. I narrowed my eyes, searching for a hidden threat within my bedroom window. The black behind the curtains was like a widening mouth ready to swallow me whole. Somewhere in the recesses of my mind, a hissing voice called, *"N-o-r-a . . . N-o-r-a!"*

"Hey, Nora!"

I screamed, digging my nails into my chest. "Declan!" I shouted. "You scared the living daylight out of me. I think I've had just about enough of that today."

"I'm sorry," he said, laughing. "I really sent the fright right into ya." He thumbed over his shoulder. "I parked around back. My da sent me ta stock the shed wit' a few more bundles of peat in case ya decide ta set a fire in the living room fireplace. Ya weren't in, so I went ahead and unloaded. Did ya go down ta the shore?"

I sighed, calming myself. Everything was better when Declan was around. "Yeah, I hadn't been down there yet. I saw Landan."

"Landan?" He scrunched his face.

Maybe he and Landan aren't friends anymore.

"He freaked me out about that window."

Declan glanced around. "Is he gone?"

I nodded.

"How come ya haven't gone ta shut that window?"

"I was sort of"—I gave him a timid smile—"afraid to go up there."

His brows pressed together. "Why?"

"I don't know. Skeletons in the closet?" I winked.

He chuckled. "I'll go wit' ya."

"Thanks."

A faint whisper cried, "*N-o-r-a.*"

What was that?

My shoulders tensed.

"Are ya a'right?" Declan leaned toward me, capturing my gaze.

I shrugged, shaking it off. "Yes, fine."

It was nothing.

6

Upstairs

"I almost forgot," I said, rifling through the grocery bags I hadn't unloaded. "I need to charge my phone."

"Lucky I put the milk away," Declan said. "Otherwise, it'd still be in that mess of bags gettin' warm."

I chortled. "If you can call what the Irish have refrigerators."

"What!" He tsked, his mouth cocking to the side.

"What? They're *so* small."

"Yah. We don't need those skyscrapers yous Americans call refrigerators. We shop more than once a month like normal people. Keeps the food fresher."

"Whatever." I smirked. "I'm hardly American. I was born here, remember?" I elbowed his ribs, then connected my phone to the charger.

"American." He jabbed back with a chuckle. He pointed toward the hallway door. "Got the keys for the stairs?"

"Yep." I wandered over to the coffee table, grabbed the keys, and tossed them to Declan.

He caught them, then shot me a cocky smile. "Shall we go release some skeletons?"

"I guess." I rolled my eyes, joining him as he opened the door to the hallway.

I loved how we bantered. It was almost as though no space and time had separated us. Only, I couldn't help but fawn over how his eyes sparkled when he smiled. I never noticed that before. Maybe because there used to be so much hair in eyes.

I'd been reluctant to explore more of the house. Now I was unsure why. Old oil paintings of the sea still decorated the hallway. I peeked into my parents' old bedroom. Nothing there remained the same. A new four poster bed with a red duvet and fancy decorative pillows sat against the back wall. A dresser and a nightstand were the only other additions. Too sterile. Too clean. I sighed and moved on.

We passed the door to the stairs, and I crossed into my grandparents' room. It was larger but shared the same look as the other one—except for the teal duvet and pillows.

"I always loved how my grandparents had such a big window in their room," I said, approaching it and gazing at the sunlight ripples on the sea.

"You going to stay in this room, then?"

"I don't know." I stared out the window, peering out at the cliff's edge. "Oh yeah, I still need to get my things. I left them at Don's."

"Ah, not ta worry. We can swing by on our way ta supper. My ma's excited ta have ya."

I grinned, warmed by the idea of his mom having dinner ready for us. That wasn't how my house had been. My mom was loving, but she didn't cook. We ate out a lot, or I made my own food. She and my dad were always busy with work, and I was always busy with track and my schoolwork. It was important to my dad that I went to university.

Checked that box off, I guess.

It didn't used to be that way, though. Not when we'd lived with my grandparents.

"Come on," Declan said, leaving the room and unlocking the door to the stairwell. The familiar creaks and croaks from the steps made me smile.

At least some things stay the same.

I followed after him.

The stairs were no longer carpeted and had the same laminate as the rest of the house. I missed the romance novels my gran used to have piled up on the stairs. When I was little, I laughed at all the *Fabio*-looking covers and asked Gran what it was about these long-haired muscle men that she loved so much. She'd just wink with a shrug and say, "When yer old enough ta gab about boys, you'll understand."

I don't think I'll ever understand.

I shook my head. The cover models were so over-the-top and ridiculous.

I reached the top of the stairs, and the ugliest piece of art my grandmother owned stared back at me. "Can't believe *this* is still here." I twisted my mouth at the hideous turquoise and red clown that hung on the wall. It looked like it'd been crafted from fish tank rocks. I'd never understood what my gran liked about it. "Why didn't this get tossed in the bins?"

Declan laughed, gawking at it too. "It really is awful. We kept a lot of stuff like this actually, but we put the rest of it in boxes for yer ma ta go t'rough."

The mention of my mom shot through me like a sobering bolt. My voice dry, I replied, "Yeah." Mom wouldn't ever go through those boxes. My face flushed, and I lowered my eyes.

"What's wrong? Did I say somethin'?"

I shook my head and moved toward my old bedroom. A cold gust of wind blew across my face from the open window. Declan crossed the room ahead of me and closed it. I shivered, rubbing my arms.

"That should stay closed now," Declan said, pushing extra hard to ensure the window stayed shut.

My bed hadn't changed. The same patchwork quilt my great-grandmother made covered it. A waft of cigarette smoke hit my nose when I sat down. "Smells like Gran up here." I scanned the room. "Everything's in boxes."

"Same in the other room, too. Two beds and a lot of boxes. I t'ink yer gran's old sewing machine is in there as well."

I smiled as Declan plopped down next to me on the edge of the bed. "I should have come up here straight away. I would have felt much better about everything. This feels like home. Even with the boxes."

"Do ya want ta look t'rough them?"

"Maybe la—"

I stood. My old bookshelf peeked out from behind some boxes. I shoved the boxes aside and chuckled. The books were still there—my favorite amongst them. I pulled it from the shelf and rubbed my fingers over the dingy, worn hardback cover.

"Is that your book?"

"My gran used to read these to me. This one was my favorite. Collection of old classic fairy tales." I opened the pages and spied an illustration of Hansel and Gretel wandering through the creepy forest. The pictures were old watercolor illustrations from the 1940s. Declan tilted his head as if waiting for me to explain. "I hated to read, but I loved to look at the pictures."

"I was the same." He reached out his hand. "Can I look at it?"

"Sure." I handed him the book.

I turned back to the shelf, running my finger over the books' spines, hoping to find my other favorite story, *David and the Phoenix.*

It's here somewhere.

I puffed through my lips, not finding it. Declan thumbed through the pages of the fairy tale book like he would discover something about me I'd never told him. My heart fluttered at the sparkle in his eye, as his smile curved higher on the right.

I lowered onto the floor, leaned back on my hands, and crossed my legs. "What are you studying at university?"

His gaze lifted to meet mine, his fingers still turning the page. "Business. I'll be done in the spring, though."

"Do you have any plans with your degree?"

He nodded. Hair fell onto his forehead and he swept it back. "Take over my da's shop."

"Really?"

He shrugged. "I like it here."

"Don't want to go into business for yourself or anything?"

He sighed, sitting up taller. "I don't know. Maybe someday. My da isn't makin' me take over his business or anythin'. If I didn't want ta, I could do something else. But it's somethin' for now, ya know?"

I nodded. He seemed so calm about the future. He wasn't fighting with the world, but rather seemed to be letting it come to him.

"I wish I could be like that," I said.

"Like what?"

"I don't know." I leaned forward, my arms on my lap. My hands twisted together. "You don't seem . . . worried."

"I don't need ta be, do I?"

I dropped my head. "No."

"How about you? What're you studyin'?"

"I'm in my second year, but I haven't picked a major. Keep changing my mind. I got a partial scholarship for track—so I went."

"Ya run track?"

I nodded with a grin. "I won state my senior year of high school for the 400-meter."

"Yer fast then."

I winked. "I've always been good at running. Wanna race?"

"Not particularly." He chuckled. "Is that why ya got those blue runnin' shoes on?"

I laughed, unfolding my legs and rolling them back and forth, showing off my shoes. "Love these shoes," I said, admiring the dark-blue stripe decorating the side. "I worked extra hours at The Corner Market Deli to get them."

"Ya worked at a deli?"

"Part-time during school. Ever need a sandwich, I'm your girl."

"Noted." His eyes stayed on mine for a moment. "So, ya don't know what ya want ta do?"

I shook my head and pursed my lips. "I think I only went because I had a scholarship, and it would get me away from Chicago. Plus, my dad seemed keen to pay for it. So, I let him." I rolled my eyes, grimacing. "I hate Chicago. But that was where we moved because it was good for my dad's"—I made air quotes with my fingers—"business." My lips twisted as a rush of anger heated my temples.

His brows drew together, and he tilted his head. "Ya never really got on wit' yer da."

"Nope." I wasn't ashamed to admit it. "He never really tried—"

I stopped. Something on the floor caught my eye. My brows pinched, and I got up for a closer look. It was a small, wooden cross lying crooked amongst a pile of wooden beads. I picked it up. "This is my gran's rosary." A flash of her rubbing the beads kindled in my mind. Her voice echoed, *Pray to Saint Mary to protect ya. Don't let the sluagh say yer name.*

"*N-o-r-a!*"

My heart leapt into my throat. "Did you hear that?" I squeaked. I eyed the windows, just as they clanged together. I jumped and held the rosary to my chest. Declan sprang to his feet.

"Sure it was nothin'," Declan said, eyes wide.

Bang. Bang.

The windows pounded again, shuddering like someone tried to shake them open.

"It's just the wind," Declan reassured, grabbing hold of

my arm. His brows lifted and his eyes widened with obvious concern.

Bang.

We jumped again at the violent clangor.

The wind howled louder, and the windows rattled with fiercer intensity. Like an invisible intruder wanted to break in. The knob slowly lifted from its latch.

Fear put my feet to flight. Declan had my arm in his grasp, pulling me out of the room and down the stairs. He locked the door to the stairwell, then scrambled down the hall with me in tow till we reached the living room.

Loud, vibrating pings rolled through the room. My adrenaline surged, and the sudden noise jolted me. We both screamed.

My eyes landed on my phone. It lit up with messages.

"Daft mobile phone!" Declan smacked his forehead.

I clutched my chest, still catching my breath. I peered back down the hallway. All the warnings from Landan earlier turned cartwheels in my stomach. Gran's rosary was in my fist.

"What was that at the window?"

Declan ran his hand down his face. "It had ta be the wind," he said, looking out the front window. He squinted through the glass. "The wind's not even blowin' hard enough for that window ta be bangin' like that. Maybe those windows need ta be replaced."

I didn't want to think it, but . . . maybe it wasn't the wind.

Declan must have seen the distress etched on my face because he placed his hand on my shoulder and gave it a good squeeze. "It wasn't anyt'ing. Ya know that, right? It's mad here by the sea. And wit' old windows . . ." He gestured toward the stairs.

I nodded. That was reasonable. I mean, what did I think? That the house was haunted? There was no such thing as the sluagh, or the Demon King Balor. None of it could be true. I was just freaking out.

"Come on. Let's go ta Don's."

I wanted Declan to convince me that it was nothing, but his wary eyes told me the event upstairs had frightened him as well. His pupils were dilated as he urged me out the door.

"Yeah," I said. "Let me get my phone."

It vibrated in my palm as I picked it up. I sighed. It was my dad. Message after message:

"Did you get to school alright?"

"Hey, haven't heard from you—I just want to know you made it."

"I know things are difficult right now. I think we need to talk."

"I know we fought on the way to the airport. I'm not mad. I just don't know what to do without your mom."

"If you could just text me a thumbs up, then I would know you're okay."

A radiant heat flooded up my neck and into my cheeks. There were some missed calls from him too. I wasn't ready to deal with this.

Why can't he just leave me alone?

I didn't want him to worry. That would lead to him finding out where I was. I went to my settings and turned my location off, sent a thumbs up, and set my phone on the countertop.

I faced Declan. "Probably need to let it charge more. I'll just leave it here."

"Right, come on," he said, motioning his hand toward the doorway.

I shot a final glance at my phone, then toward the upstairs window, and followed Declan out the door.

7

Chasing Fear

"Let's get some chips." Declan rolled my suitcase down the hallway at Pete's Pub & Inn.

"Isn't your mom making us supper?"

Declan shrugged. "Awe, come on. It will be like old times. Besides, we don't have ta tell my ma we had 'em."

"It might spoil my appetite," I teased.

"Nah, come on. A few chips won't hurt nothin'. We'll split an order."

I grinned and couldn't help but think he was right. Eating chips together was the best idea he'd had all day.

"Don will be glad ta have ya a little while longer, anyway. Did ya see the look on his face when we came ta get yer t'ings? Thought he might cry."

I laughed. "I hardly think he was that upset."

"Oh, he was." Declan winked.

"Well, then, let's get some chips with extra seasoning."

"Ya remembered," he said, leading the way down the stairs.

"It really is the best way to have them. You know, I think he puts sugar in his spice mix."

"There's something in that spice I can't get enough of." We hit the bottom of the stairwell, then out into the pub. "I'll load this in the car. You get us a table."

I nodded. Don grinned at me from behind the bar, already pointing out a perfect spot for us to sit.

"It's just like old times," he said as he walked over, planting an extra-large helping of chips at our table.

My eyes widened. "Had them ready, huh?"

"Course, gurl." Don winked. The hostess, Tracy, walked by with a grin. Don leaned closer. "She wouldn't have given ya the extra chips if I hadn't done it."

Tracy hollered over her shoulder, "Paintin' me as the bad guy again, Don?"

Don snickered in response as Declan reentered the pub and joined me at our table.

"I still have to eat supper, Don," I said, staring at the heaping portion of fries.

"Ya come to Pete's"—Don waved his fingers above the fries like he was doing a magic trick—"you get a load of gold. Now, eat 'em up. Yer stomach will be fine for supper. Who doesn't have extra room for chips?"

"See?" Declan chimed with a twinkle in his eyes.

"It's like you two had this planned," I said.

Don thrust a white towel over his shoulder and sauntered back behind the bar with a knowing grin.

Declan took the first chip. "Oh, hot," he huffed, fanning his hand over his mouth.

"It's easy to forget just how hot those dang things are until it's too late." I picked up a fry and blew on it. An unsettled feeling wriggled back into my gut, and I lowered the fry. "Don't you think that was weird at the house—what happened with the windows?"

"I'm tellin' ya. I know it was a bit jarring, but it was just the wind."

"I know, I know," I said, trying to convince myself.

"Still put the fear of God inta me for a quick minute."

I doubled over with laughter. "We were both off like a shot."

"Those track lessons came in handy for ya." He chuckled. "Dodged right out of there. Really daft of me ta panic like that."

"I used to believe in all those ghost stories Gran used to tell me. They really freaked me out. Some of that rushed through my mind when the windows started banging."

"I know, it's like it came out of nowhere."

My brows scrunched, and I popped the fry into my mouth. "Nora? What's wrong?"

"It's just—" I hesitated, the words trapped on my tongue.

"What?" He leaned forward with a concerned look.

"I thought the wind said my name."

Declan smirked like I was foolish.

"I know, I think my mind was playing tricks on me." I didn't want Declan to think I was crazy. And I definitely wasn't going to mention the other times I thought I'd heard it.

"The sluagh aren't real. Neither are banshees or Balor. None of them," Declan said with a condescending tone that made me feel dumb.

"I'm not an idiot."

His mouth fell open, and he held up his hands. "No—sorry, Nora. I didn't mean it that way. Ya just seem ta have a look in yer eye, like ya need ta be reminded."

"Yeah, well . . . maybe I do," I conceded.

Don came back over with two pints. "Ya aren't children anymore. Don't need lemonades wit' yer chips, and maybe somethin' heartier than tea. It's half-five. Time for a pint."

"Cheers, Don," Declan said, reaching for his wallet.

"On the house, boy. Happy ta see the two of yous together again." Don winked over his shoulder as he sauntered away.

I pressed my lips together and stared at the table.

"Come on, Nora. Tell me what yer t'inkin."

"You know when you're a kid," I said, "and you're walking home in the dark, and then suddenly you get this feeling there's something behind you, so you start walking faster. You *know* there is nothing back there, but the faster you walk, the more afraid you become. Before you know it, you're running for the door, sure a monster is about to grab you."

Declan stared at me as if waiting to hear where I was going with this.

"Anyway . . . it's like you can't get your grip on the handle fast enough. You jump through the door and slam it behind you. Only to laugh at yourself because there was never anything there."

"Yah," he said, as though still waiting for the point.

"It's irrational."

"Right," he agreed.

"But still, you can't keep yourself from being afraid when you're running." Something about what I said dried my throat, and I took a giant gulp of my beer.

Declan's eyes narrowed, and he reached across the table toward my hand, but then stopped and set his palm on the table. "Nora"—he leaned closer—"when are ya goin' ta tell me what you're runnin' from?"

I wish I knew.

I considered telling him all the things that I thought it could be, but the lump in my throat cautioned me. I wish he'd just grabbed my hand instead. I needed some reassurance that everything would be okay. I'd come home to escape. Declan was right. It was like he could see it in my eyes. I was a girl running as fast—and as far—as I could.

But what am I running from?

I had run home because of Mom—because of Gran. They weren't here. Instead, there was something else.

8

Toppling Stones

"So did my sister get any stories out of ya?" Declan asked as he drove me back to the house.

Dinner had been phenomenal—Patty cooked a roast with homemade brown bread. Seeing Patty again had been wonderful, though it was Della who had monopolized my time.

"Well"—I shot Declan a mischievous grin—"I tried to come up with some of the worst things we did when we were little. None of them seemed to satisfy what she was after, though."

"The stories Della's looking for aren't the ones ya would've told her, anyway."

Huh?

"What do you mean?"

"She's wantin' to know if we ki—" He rolled his shoulders. "Never mind Della."

"Well, I didn't tell her about the time we snuck out to explore the caves and almost drowned. She might have been satisfied with that one."

Declan tsked. "Oh, my da never lets me forget about that one. Della's heard that story already, anyway."

"I was glad your dad found us that day. He was furious, but my dad would've been—" I looked out the window. "My dad would've never let me see you again. I was *so* relieved when your dad covered for me. All my parents knew was that we'd gone for a swim in our clothes again."

I turned back toward Declan. He seemed tense, glaring ahead at the road.

"You okay?" I asked.

"Should've never happened. That whole t'ing was my fault."

I swiped my hand, brushing it off. "It was a long time ago, and it was hardly your fault."

The muscles in Declan's jaw twitched.

"I was the one that suggested we do it. If it was anyone's fault, it was mine. I didn't always think things through when I was twelve." I shrugged. "I guess I still don't."

Declan shook his head, his lips tightening. "I knew that cave flooded, but I wanted ta impress ya." He shuddered. "Still remember reaching for yer hand when that current tugged ya under."

Declan's hand, reaching for mine in the blue swirl of water, was the last thing I'd seen before going under—the gap between our hands growing wider and wider.

And the bracelet—

An uncomfortable ache struck my chest.

Declan's fingers had pulled it from my wrist as his grip broke loose. The bracelet was a simple leather string pulled through a small whelk shell. Nothing special, except that it was from Declan. I lost it to the churning sea.

I lost more than I thought I had that day. I've thought of that bracelet often.

"I thought you were gone forever," he said, eyes flaring. "I don't t'ink I've ever felt more scared in my life. You were just gone. Swallowed up by that black water." A breath appeared to catch in his chest. "I'll *never* let myself be that reckless again. If it weren't for ya grabbing hold of that rock . . . "

"Declan," I said, trying to call him back from the trauma he'd clearly been carrying all these years.

He flicked his eyes at me, then back at the road.

"I'm so sorry, Dec." She let the old nickname for him slip. "Here I was thinking it was just something we'd gotten away with—I didn't know it affected you so much. I know we were lucky to have lived, but . . . it was you that pulled me out."

"Yah, well . . . " He sniffed. His eyes glistened. He swiped his arm across his face. "Yer dad ended up taking ya away not long after that, anyway."

I hated that day.

"I know," I whispered. Again, the need to apologize for my dad taking us away ate at me.

The memory resurged of my dad pulling me into the car. Declan stood just far enough away, his eyes full of tears, my dad like a wall between us as he dragged me from our doorway into the car. "Dad, *please.* Just let me see him. He's my friend. Let me say goodbye." Tears flooded down my face as I struggled, trying to get a glimpse of Declan. I don't know why Dad was in such a hurry. I wished I could've lived with Lem and Patty. I'd screamed, *"I hate you,"* at my dad. It'd made no difference. He didn't stop or turn around, just drove us farther and farther away from the only place we'd called home.

Leaving my home—and Declan—was something I'd never come to grips with. Apparently, neither had Declan.

I didn't know I'd meant so much to him.

Coming here, I wasn't even sure he'd recognize me.

Tears welled in my eyes. I was glad he never forgot. Glad he was here now. Everything in me wanted to set my hand over his. So tempting. Declan's hand was just there, resting over the gear shift.

The tires rolled over gravel, pulling me out of my thoughts. I wiped away my single tear before Declan noticed as we pulled up to The Flaherty House. I put my hand on the door, ready to exit the car, but hesitated. Declan's lack of movement captured my attention. His eyes were wide.

"What is it?" I asked. He didn't budge. I followed his gaze and—

Chills skittered up my spine.

There ahead of us, as Declan pulled the parking brake, was the yawning open window of the upstairs bedroom. The curtains flailed in the wind.

"What the hell?" Declan opened his car door and charged toward the house.

"Declan?" I called. He unlocked the door and disappeared into the house. I got out of the car, but hesitated.

Do I even want to go in there?

Meow.

Buttons's black shadow caught my eye as he dashed across the thatched roof, then leapt behind the house. The blackness of the open door loomed like a ghostly void. My stomach dropped. I closed my eyes, trying to shake off the fear.

Wind whistled past my ears. *"N-o-r-a!"*

"Declan?"

"N-o-r-a!"

The loose curls around my face flailed in front of my eyes as I spun toward the sea. The lighthouse was dark. No light emanated from its beams of safety. I gritted my teeth, plugged my ears, and burst toward the house. I'd had enough. I refused to listen.

I crossed the threshold, flipped on the lights, then shut the door behind me. I gasped for breath, whispering to myself, "It's only the wind. Just the wind." I stared at the door as if any moment it would burst open.

The *click* of a door behind me sent panic through my blood. I spun around just as Declan walked through the hallway door.

"It's just me. It's okay!" he reassured me.

I slammed into his chest and clung to him for dear life. My fingers curled into his back.

He squeezed me tight, his cheek resting on top of my head. "It's okay." He held me back to look at me, setting his hands on my shoulders. "You're tremblin'." He rubbed his hands over my arms as though it might help calm me. "It was just the cat. He must have pushed the window open. I caught him lying on yer bed. I chased the daft cat away. The latch just needs to be fixed. That's all." His eyes held my gaze, as if trying to determine if I believed him.

My name whispered in the wind entered my thoughts.

Should I tell him I heard it again? No. He'll think I'm losing it.

"Don't go," I said instead.

"Course." He grinned, his shoulders relaxing as though glad I'd asked.

I sighed, relieved I wouldn't be alone. Though dread still lingered as I stared through the hallway door.

"No need to be afraid of a cat." He gave my arms a final squeeze, then escorted me to the sofa. "Ya want some tea? Maybe that will calm ya down."

I nodded.

"Hey. Yer safe." He knelt in front of me. His beautiful green eyes stared into mine. I couldn't help but grin. "There ya are." He smiled back. He brushed his fingers through my loose curls and tucked them behind my ear.

A warm feeling shot through me like whisky. Something new kindled—a strong, impulsive wish that blasted past my fears. I wanted him closer. His hand lingered on my cheek, and his musky, peppermint scent washed over me like a memory of our time on the shore.

"It's cold in here." He got up and wandered down the hallway, returning with an armful of duvets, one from each of the beds. He tossed the teal one on the recliner, then wrapped the red one around my shoulders.

"There. Now, how about I get a fire started and put the kettle on?"

"Thanks, Declan."

"And I won't leave. Not unless ya want me to."

My fright melted away in the warmness of his smile. So long as Declan was with me, I didn't have anything to worry about.

"You start the fire, I'll get the tea going," I said. "Stupid window scared the hell out of me, but I'm not an invalid."

"Course, ya aren't. Yer a track star, even if it had been somet'in' real, you'd have outrun it."

I chuckled. "Yeah, I suppose so. You want tea?"

"Yes, please." He knelt next to the fireplace and loaded in some peat.

I kept the blanket tight around me and got up to fill the kettle with water. "Should probably turn the heater on while I'm up."

"Yah, probably," he hollered back. "But it's still nice ta have the fire goin'."

"No argument there."

My phone pinged as I ambled into the kitchen. It was lit up with more messages and missed calls. I refused to even look at it. Declan was with me, and I wasn't about to let Dad ruin our time. Not right now, anyway.

I filled the kettle and clicked it on. Declan had already kicked his shoes off and now sat in the recliner, buried under the duvet with his feet raised. The fire crackled, casting an orange glow on the living room furniture. I waited for the water to boil and filled our cups. The steam from our mugs wafted to my nose, warming my cheeks. I shuffled back into the living room, balancing one mug in each hand—all while holding the blanket up with my arms.

"Here you go?" I twittered.

He grinned and took the mug. I snuggled onto the couch with mine.

"I'm really glad to see you again, Declan."

He blew into his mug and took a careful first sip. "Do ya really t'ink you'll stay?"

I shrugged. "I don't know."

"What about school?"

"I don't know about that either." I stared into my tea, not wanting to consider any of it. I needed more time. But then, none of my time in the States felt like it belonged to me, anyway. Could I go to university here? My mom was Irish, plus I was born here—my dad American. I had dual citizenship.

I swallowed a sip of my tea. "You know, I never wanted to leave in the first place. Though I won't be able to stay in this house. I can't afford to pay for it unless Della wants to give me a job. My dad won't keep paying the bills without renters. He'd discover something was up. He's been wanting to sell for a while, but Mom hasn't let him."

"Ya gotta tell yer parents, Nora."

The void Mom left pricked my grief.

Just Dad. Hold it together.

I kept silent, working to control my emotions. Not telling Declan was like an anvil threatening to drag me to the floor, but would grief devour me if I let it out?

"I know. I don't want to tell . . . Dad yet. He'll just try to make me come home. Worse yet, he'll come to get me."

Declan's face dropped. "He can't do that. Not unless ya let him."

I groaned. "He ruined my life once. He'll do it again."

"No." Declan shook his head, then repeated, "Not unless ya let him. You're not twelve anymore. He can't just throw you in the back of the car this time."

Why doesn't that feel true? Why does it feel like he can?

Sadness threatened to creep back over me. Thoughts of

my mom shook the fragile stability I clung to so desperately. Declan's eyes searched my face as if looking for the full story. I wanted to tell him, but I didn't want to fall apart. I wasn't ready for that.

"Remember when yer gran had just passed away, and ya ran away," he said *so* knowingly.

I nodded.

"I'd set a fire on the shore, just like this one, and you and I huddled in a blanket next to it. Our parents never figured out where our secret fort was. It was a good place to hide." He paused, tapping his fingers against his mug. "I remember knowing everyt'ing was about ta change. I held ya so close, hoping I was wrong. Yer da and mum were searchin' for ya, and we stayed hidden until mornin'."

A breath caught in my chest, and my eyes filled with tears. My voice wavered as I said, "My dad was so mad when he found us."

"I'm sorry," he said. "I don't want ta upset ya."

"It's okay," I said, wishing Declan's arm was around me, just like it'd been that day when we were twelve.

"I used ta wish we'd hidden somewhere else. Somewhere they wouldn't have been able ta find us. I vowed that if I ever saw ya again—" He stopped himself and bit his bottom lip. "I still can't believe yer here."

I gazed at him, blinking away tears. "This was the only place I could think to come."

Declan set his tea down and joined me on the sofa. "Come here ta me," he said, wrapping his arm around me and pulling me to his side. "I don't know what happened ta ya, but I'm here when ya want ta tell me."

I could only cry in response, glad I wasn't alone. I lay with my ear against his chest, his warmth lulling me into a place of safety. I just wanted to stay next to him. I couldn't believe I was here, and he was here with me. The fire licked peacefully, and Declan remained unmoved until I fell asleep.

The house was still warm when I opened my eyes. I was on the sofa but on my side with a pillow under my head. Dull morning light peeked through the front windows.

Where is Declan? Did he move to the recliner?

I lifted my head. He wasn't there. I yawned, rubbing the sleep out of my eyes.

A fire still burned in the fireplace. If Declan left, he hadn't been gone for long.

I sat up with a groan. A strange sore spot ached in my hip. I reached into my pocket and pulled out my gran's rosary. It'd been stabbing into my hip all night. I fondled the wooden beads for a moment, admiring the simplicity of the shiny cross, then set it on the coffee table. I grimaced, rubbing the soreness out of my hip.

"Declan," I called in a weak, groggy voice. No reply. The shower down the hallway wasn't running either.

I got up, still wrapped in my blanket, and peered out the window. Declan's car was gone, and a thick layer of fog obscured the ground.

"Huh?"

Where would he have gone?

The tea from last night sat cold on the table. I moved to retrieve the mugs and spied a note. I snatched it up.

Nora,

Sorry I had to run out. I didn't want to wake you. Figured you needed rest. I have a few classes this morning in Donégal, but I will be back this afternoon. Hope you don't mind if I swing back by when I get back to the carraig. Been brilliant having you back, and I wanted to talk to you about something.

Oh, and . . . just stay out of the upstairs. Keep it locked until I can get my da to come look at it. I'm pretty sure that latch is broke, and I want to keep that cat out of there. I don't want you afraid to sleep here. If it keeps being a problem, we can put you back up at Don's, or even my parents' house. We'll all take care of you.

Declan

"We'll all take care of you." I read that line again out loud and smiled. I hadn't been taken care of by anyone in a long time. I'd lived more independently—more alongside my parents than with them. It had worked for us, I suppose. But that was what stung the most after Mom died. I wished I'd spent more time with her. I wished I could've seen her one last time before—

I shook my head, drawing in a steady breath.

No tears. Not today.

I needed to settle in a bit more. Forget about things. Enjoy the sea.

That's if this fog lifts. Can't see anything right now.

The misty blanket kept drifting along, as if it had no intention of leaving and lifting my mood.

I didn't want to sit here and wait for Declan. My mind would drag me down in the silence if I did. The shops were only a couple miles up the road, and it would be a straight shot.

I'll go for a run, then get coffee and breakfast at Della's afterward.

Running always helped lift my spirits.

I ate a small piece of toast, then got myself geared up for a run, complete with my green hoodie, black track bottoms, and blue runners. I pulled a gray beanie over my curls, then went out the door for a quick warm up and stretch before running up the gravel drive. The wooden post appeared through the fog, indicating a right turn onto the main road. I kept to the side along the rope fence that was a barrier between the road and the cliffs that overlooked the sea.

The fog was dense, but just clear enough for me to navigate a few steps ahead. The cool air wafted into my lungs, energizing my strides. I focused on the ground all the way across the long opening until the sidewalk appeared ahead of me. Now that I was on the main drag, the shops on my right kept the fog from clouding my view. Other morning villagers bustled through the dense white that surrounded everything. It wasn't long before I came upon Della's pink door.

I paused to catch my breath. The run had been a good choice. I smiled as I pushed open the door, and the rush of warm air melted my cold cheeks.

"Nora!" came Della's welcome from behind the espresso bar. She had the cutest pink flower barrette peeking out from behind her left ear.

"Hi." I waved with a smile, skipping over to the counter.

"Did you run in that fog?"

"Yeah." I winked. "It's not so bad. I knew where I was going." I glanced at her pastry case. This time, the sausage rolls abounded. I pointed at them. "But I bet one of those sausage rolls would help warm me up real quick. As well as one of your perfect lattes." I lowered my gaze. "Gran always loved the sweet drinks. She would've wanted something with vanilla and caramel if your shop had been around back then."

Della grinned. "Happy ta get them for ya." She swiped my card and got to work gathering my order. "It's been a slow mornin'. The fog keeps people in unless they have somewhere ta go." She rolled her eyes and put her hands on her hips. "Like having ta come ta work at the café I begged my da for."

I laughed. "I'll keep you company for a little while. No need to rush back. Declan has classes this morning, anyway."

"Oh?" she said with an inquiring lilt. "Declan, eh?"

Why'd I say that?

I took a deep breath, working to conceal the blush that tried to redden my cheeks. "Come on, Della."

"Come on yerself. Don't pretend yer not happy ta see him. I mean . . . ya know he's been pining after ya all these years. No gurl has ever been good enough for him in comparison ta you."

"Della, it's not like that. We're just friends."

She shook her head and chuckled. "Please now, Nora. I might be only nineteen, but even I know better. Yer tellin' me ya never kissed him . . . or ever wanted ta?"

"I never . . . I mean . . . " My cheeks heated as I thought about his green eyes from the night before. "It's never been like that is all."

"Sure," she said with a wily grin, setting my pastry on a plate in front of me. She turned to make my espresso. "Ya should've seen yer face when ya first set eyes on him yesterday."

Did I make a face? Was it that obvious?

I touched my cheeks.

Am I doing it now?

"Della," I groaned, hoping she would change the subject.

"Right, right, I'll leave ya alone about it." She winked at me, pouring another latte with an intentional heart shape in the milky froth, then handed it to me. "I'll stop botherin' ya about it. I just like fishin' ta find somet'ing I can get under Declan's skin wit'. He's always so cool and unbothered. Needs a good shakin' up. Come on, let's sit down."

She grabbed my plate and motioned over to a window table. I sat down with my latte. Della scooted my sausage roll toward me. The first warm bite of flaky puff pastry was delectable. I stared out the window into the foggy, white nothingness while savoring the mouthful. "Gosh, I haven't had one of these in years."

"Ya don't have these in the States?"

"No—and I wish we did. There is nothing like them."

Della smiled, watching me eat. "Be so grand if ya stayed. I'd have a friend right here in the village."

"You don't have any friends here?"

"Not really. I mean, I have friends that I went ta school wit' that aren't far away, but they aren't here in the carraig. I don't see them as often now that I am a busy slavin' at my café. Saving for a car. I might see them more often once I have one."

"Are you going to go to university?"

She shrugged. "Maybe. Love ta go to culinary school someday for bakin', but right now, I kinda like doin' this."

"I don't blame you. It's nice here."

"I like being by the sea, plus I still can practice my bakin' here from home. Loads of experts you can learn from online nowadays."

A smile tugged at my lips. "That's true."

"Soon I will be makin' my own sausage rolls, instead of havin' them delivered in from the bakery up the road." Her eyes floated upward as though picturing the whole thing.

"Well, if I do stay, I would have a hard time not coming here every day for a coffee." I took a sip of the creamy milk, its golden foam floating atop my latte. "This is so good."

"Irish aren't really known for their coffee, but wit' the right beans and know-how, it isn't that hard ta make a good one."

Lem walked into the café and sauntered over to us. "Good mornin', Nora."

"Good morning."

"How did ya get over here?"

"I went for a run."

"In the fog?" he asked, his brows scrunching.

"I asked her the same t'ing. Apparently, the fog doesn't bother her," Della said.

I laughed. "I run a lot in the mornings. I'm used to bad weather. Besides, it was a straight shot. It wasn't hard."

"Well, aren't ya the adventurous one," Lem said, scratching his head as though unsure he agreed it was the safest thing for a young woman to do.

"Maybe I should buy a book from your shop. As long as it's foggy like this, I might need something to pass the time."

"Come on over," he said, swiping his arm toward the bookcase. "Yes, let's get ya somet'in' ta keep ya indoors where it's nice and toasty. I got some new ones in. Some really nice journals too."

I grabbed my coffee and followed, happy to peruse the shelves with him.

"What kind of books do ya like? We got some romancy ones in from a local author down there." He pointed toward the bottom of one of the bookshelves. "Here are the journals, though. Aren't they pretty?" He grabbed a black leather journal with an embedded tree made of Celtic knots and held it up. "The tourists like these ones."

A green journal on the shelf caught my eye, so I reached for it. Some scratches on the back of the shelf stopped me halfway. "Look, Lem." I pointed. "Someone has scratched up your bookcase."

"Oh—" His face dropped, and he looked at Della, then back at me. "Em?"

Did I say something I shouldn't have?

I was about ready to change the subject when Lem said, "Let me show ya."

He grabbed a few more journals off the shelf, a heart with initials inside now on full display.

L.P. + U.F. Forever

I pressed my brows together, waiting for him to explain.

"Those are mine and yer mum's initials."

"What?" I took a step back, my mouth falling open.

"Lemuel Patterson and Una Flaherty," he said with a grin.

"Ya know, I've known yer mum since we were kids. When we were little, I had quite the shine for her, and she for me."

"You've had these shelves that long?"

"Course. This was me da's shop before it was mine. Though it wasn't a post office or bookshop back then. It was more of a supply shop. Got quite the scolding for scratchin' up his shelves. I had to go fetch a twitch for that one." He rubbed the back of his hands as though remembering the sting of the lashes.

I hissed through my teeth. "Was it worth it?"

He lifted his eyes to the initials and grinned. "A hundred times."

I nodded, taking in the information.

"It was a good memory of yer mum and I carvin' our initials, so I just left them there. Piece of the shop's history and all." He rocked back on his heels and wrapped his arms behind his back. "Well, anyway—yer mum and I grew up, and she met James, and I met Patty." He whistled, lifting his gaze. "And Patty stole me heart away. It was meant to be."

He brought his eyes back to mine. "But, the Pattersons and Flahertys . . . I mean Morrigans"—he winked—"always stayed close, though. That was up until ya moved. Sure would love ta see Una again. She's like family around here."

I touched the heart, tracing the U initial of my mother's name with the tip of my finger.

"Una Flaherty," Lem said, shaking his head with a grin. "Miss that gurl. Always wished yer family would move on back."

We . . . she can't.

Guilt struck a powerful chord in my chest. My face heated. It wasn't right that Lem didn't know about Mom. That none of them did. But even the thought of telling him was more than my heart could bear. My breathing quickened, and my heart thudded up into my ears. Tears threatened to well in my eyes.

His expression shifted, and his mouth parted. "Is there somet'in' *wrong*, gurl?"

I took a step away from him and ran my hands over my face in hopes that it might calm me down. "I . . . " A sudden swallow of emotion stopped my voice. "Lem, I . . . " I tried again, but I couldn't make myself say the words. But I had to.

He should know. They should all know.

My dad should have told him. Why hadn't he?

"It isn't fair," I finally said, my hands balled into fists. I felt like a fish with a hook in its mouth, trying to pull the words out. "My dad . . . h–he should've told you. I didn't know where else to go, so I came here."

Lem rubbed his chin. "I don't understand ya, darlin'. What are ya tryin' ta say?"

I took a few more steps back. Dread pushed out a few tears. I turned to Della as they coasted down my cheeks, hoping, somehow, she could say it for me.

"I'm sorry . . . I'm so sorry he didn't tell you."

"Didn't tell me what?" His brows pinched tighter.

I was a volcano about to erupt. "My mom . . . she's—"

My eyes whipped over my shoulder toward the door. "Two weeks ago, she—"

"She what?" Lem took a step toward me. His hands slowly lifted. Dread seemed to quiver inside his eyes, as though the curtain had already opened to reveal the awful truth. It emanated through my skin—the horrifying reality that not even I wanted to believe was true.

"Please don—don't tell me," Lem begged.

"She died," I said, and the dam I'd worked so hard to keep at bay burst. I bent forward, setting one hand on my knee, the other struggling to hold my coffee.

Don't lose it. Keep yourself together.

"Una is dead?" Lem cried.

I peered up at Lem for a fleeting moment.

His wide eyes trembled. He stumbled back a few steps, clutching his heart. "She can't be . . . dead. How?" The disturbed look on his face sharpened the ache in my heart.

I knew the pain he felt. I couldn't help him. I couldn't even help myself.

"Same . . . as killed . . . Gran." The words choked me as they came out.

Lem stepped toward me. I ambled back. My coffee teetered from my hand and splattered onto the floor. The splash of the coffee felt like the torrent inside my chest—eating up my mind. The hot liquid mirroring my broken emotions—too big a mess to clean up.

"Nora?" Lem called through my storm.

I raced for the door, my breath heaving in my ears. The white fog enveloped me, and I bolted like I was running for my life.

"*N-o-r-a!*" the wind whispered through my tumult.

Maybe I was.

9

The Sluagh

My insides screamed as I fled, my feet pounding against the sidewalk. The awful look on Lem's face kept replaying in my mind. The fragile glass that kept the horrifying reality of my mom's death at bay shattered. I tried to pretend, but already the cliffs tumbled into the murky sea of my life.

What will I do now? I can't escape it.

I ran ahead, one sprinting step after the other, blazing a trail back for the house. I struggled to focus on my path. The blinding white fog disoriented me.

I need to calm down.

I wiped my sleeve across my eyes, blinking through the haze. I peered down at my feet. The road was on my right, but there was no fence on my left.

I must be crossing the entrance to the beach.

I narrowed my eyes, waiting for the roped fence to appear. My stomach swirled—where was it? Creeping anxiety sobered my grief. I didn't want to get lost.

My empty footfalls slowed.

Should I turn around?

But then, the first fence post emerged through the fog. I exhaled in relief.

There it is.

I picked up speed with a desperate need to escape the fog. The grinding gravel beneath my feet was a pounding cadence as I blazed ahead. Everything else lay still in an eerie silence until—

"*N-o-r-a!*"

No.

My heart squeezed. Icy tingles rushed over my skin.

"*N-o-r-a!*"

The baleful whispers spurred me faster. But the moans repeated louder, and louder. Fear hastened my stride. My eyes darted back and forth in the blinding mist, leaving me vulnerable—exposed to an invisible predator, lurking like a shark in dark water.

The voice rushed closer.

Is that heat on my neck from panic? Or from the wind's evil breath?

It called right next to my ear, "*N-o-r-a!*"

I screamed, glancing behind me.

Nothing.

The nightmarish, milky haze went on and on—my safety pushed farther and farther away from me.

Must get away. Run faster.

"*N-O-R-A!*" the voice boomed, shaking my insides. I tripped over my feet, slid across gravel, and rolled until I lay flat on my back.

"Ugh," I cried. The stings of road rash raked over my skin. My knees and elbows burned. My chin—I touched it. Red dotted my fingertips.

I cursed. My chest pulsed with sobs. Warm tears dripped down my temples.

"*N-o-r-a!*"

I bolted upright. The blank mist fell quiet. Movement in my peripheral captured my gaze. Faint fluttering drifted through the thick, vaporous swirls. Like black birds appearing and disappearing—several all at once and then nothing.

Quiet.

I struggled to control my panting breaths.

But then, a racket, like countless thrashing wings, tore around me. I covered my head. My eyes widened into the clouded brume. Black smoke mixed into the fog in thin spectral swirls.

"N-O-R-A!" the voice called again like a pounding thrum.

I held my breath, unable to move, scream, or run.

A tangle of muddy vapors, wrestling together in a tight knot, hovered in front of me. The black inky elements unfolded, revealing a large crow at my feet. Its beak pointed down at the ground. It remained still and inanimate.

My eyes flared and my throat clamped—I couldn't swallow as I stared at the tar-like phantom bird.

It snapped its beak at me, and I gasped. My heart pounded, and my fingers clenched the rocks beneath me. Its black talons tapped the gravel as it hopped closer.

"G-Get out of here," I screamed, kicking at it.

It paused, then spread its giant wings. "CAW!"

The clash of cascading wings followed its call, and I bolted, running for my life. They were behind me. The wings. The cawing and the baleful howl of my name, repeated over and over, drew closer and closer.

The wooden post—finally I turned left into the drive and kept running. The heat of fear—the adrenaline—choked my breath. I couldn't stop. It was the sluagh. I was certain of it. They called my name—they were coming to take my life like they'd done to Gran and Mom.

I sprinted for the house.

Declan.

I wished he was here. I wished I wasn't terrified and alone.

I didn't notice when my feet stopped pounding gravel

and instead beat soft, grassy turf. I would've slowed down. I would've stopped running. Panic blinded my attention until, all at once, my feet dropped off the edge of the cliff.

A pair of warm, rough hands grabbed my arms. I kicked at the air with my feet as I flung backward into a solid embrace.

I screamed, sure it was the sluagh that had gotten me. "Let go! Let go!"

"What are ya doin'?" a familiar male voice rebuked, calling me back from my terror.

I peered up at the one who had saved me. Landan's dark hair swirled around his fierce green eyes.

"Have ya lost yer mind?" he shouted. "Ya just threw yerself over the side of a cliff."

Relief flooded through my limbs, and I bent forward, gasping for breath. Black spots dotted my vision. My knees shook, my body on the verge of crumbling.

"Yer face is bleedin," Landan said, grabbing my arms and steadying me.

"I . . . I fell," I said, working to swallow down the adrenaline. "I didn't see the cliff through the fog."

"What're ya doin' out in the fog, anyway?" he asked through gritted teeth. "It's dangerous."

I glared at him and yanked my arms away.

If one more person tells me that . . .

"Well, I guess I could say the same thing to you. What the hell are you doing out here?" I pressed my shaking hand to my sweaty forehead and closed my eyes, trying to steady my emotions. The monsters seemed to have vanished, but I continued to stare behind me.

"I'm out her savin' ya from leapin' off a cliff!" he snapped.

I pursed my lips.

He threw his hands up, as if he'd had enough. "Grand! Have it yer way! I'm just glad ya didn't kill yerself."

I laid my hand on my chest, slowing my breaths. "I'm sorry. Y-You're right. I should be thanking you. If it weren't for you, I would have leapt right over that edge. Definitely not the ending I was planning for." I shot him a weak sheepish grin even though my instincts still told me to keep going until the door was closed behind me.

"What were ya doin' running so fast?"

"You wouldn't believe me."

His eyes softened. "Ya look shaken up." He tsked, shaking his head. "Come on. Ya need ta sit down. Ya hurt yerself." He offered his hand and led me to the old rickety bench my grandad had built. Another layer of fright relented as I took a seat next to him. The coolness of the bench seeped through the backs of my thighs, relaxing my nerves.

"What happened?" he asked.

My mind raced. Was I going insane? Had I really just been chased by dark shadows in the fog? That crow had been real. I was certain of that. My pulse raced faster just thinking about it.

I clenched my teeth and turned my hands over. My palms were scuffed and bleeding.

"Listen." Landan's brows curved, and he leaned in. "I can help ya if you'll let me."

What would he know about monsters? "It wasn't as though I was trying to purposely run off the cliff."

He shook his head. "That's not what I am talkin' about."

"What are you talking about then?" I threw my hands up.

"The reason you were runnin' in the first place."

I bit my lip. What was I going to say? That a flock of evil crows chased me?

"Nora. You don't need ta be afraid ta talk to me. I know all about the curse."

My eyes flared. "Curse?" The word knotted my stomach.

"Come on now." He smirked as though my reaction was ridiculous. "Yer gran told ya all about it. Ya used ta tell *me* all about it when we were kids."

"What? How could there possibly be a curse?"

A little bit of sun peeked through the fog. The faint lines of the shore appeared through the haze. Landan stared out at the sea as if considering what to say next. "Nora, t'ings are not as plain and ordinary as you'd like ta t'ink. There is more than ya can see wit' yer eyes. Invisible t'ings that are just as real as you—as Declan. And—"

He paused for a moment, twisting his lips. "There are t'ings ya don't understand about yer gran's death." He gazed at me through the corner of his eye. "Or yer ma's."

My chin quivered. "How could you possibly know about my mom?"

"Word travels fast in small villages."

"Not that fast." I shook my head, baffled. So many unexplained phenomena had been happening around me, and Landan's assertions were more than I was ready to hear. Maybe I just didn't want to believe it. I wanted him to be like Declan and tell me it was just the wind.

Curse.

I racked my brain trying to remember all the things Gran used to tell me.

I breathed a deep sigh. "My gran told me a lot of things. But I used to be the most horrified when she would talk about her sister, Aunt Nieve. She was supposedly deceived by a *gancanagh*." I rolled my eyes. "You telling me you believe shape-shifting fairies are real?"

His eyes narrowed as he stared out at the sea.

I followed his gaze toward the lighthouse, but it wasn't visible through the fog. "Gran also said that Balor saw Nieve because of the gancanagh, and that he sent the sluagh after her."

Landan's deep voice hummed. "I doubt the truth was that simple. T'ings are called names by people who don't understand the world of spirits and devils."

My insides quaked at his words. "What if—what if the sluagh are real?"

"Do ya t'ink they're real, Nora?"

I sniffed. "You're going to just think I'm crazy if I say yes."

He looked me square in the eye. His intense gaze caught me off guard. Something in it seemed to stare past my eyes and into my soul. "Nora, I can help ya. You *just* need ta trust me."

"Help me?"

His piercing gaze gave me no room to retreat.

"Okay, okay," I murmured. "This might seem crazy. I mean, really, really mad."

His stare seemed to say, *"Try me."*

I nodded. "I keep hearing my name. Like . . . like someone is calling to me from"—I gazed down at my hands—"the sea."

Landan didn't say anything, so I went on. "I tried to ignore it. But just now—*just now*—I heard it again. But this time it was so loud." My hands started to shake, so I folded them together. "And then—"

I stopped, searching for the best way to explain it. "Something came after me." My voice rose into a higher pitch. "It was the sluagh."

Landan grabbed my wrist, and his face grew serious. "Ya have ta listen ta me very carefully, Nora. Yer Aunt Nieve wouldn't have died if yer gran had never meddled."

Gran's fault?

My breath hitched. "What?"

"You'll be safe, but you'll need ta trust me. Can ya do that?"

"You believe me?"

The fact that he didn't even flinch frightened me. He looked over his shoulder at the house—now visible through the haze. "There are t'ings ya don't know, Nora."

"But you do?" I challenged.

His mysterious eyes turned back to mine, and I held my breath. His hand was still locked around my wrist. I glanced down at his white knuckles, then met his eyes. An ethereal otherness teemed inside them. He'd seen things I hadn't. Maybe I did need to trust him.

He pointed at the house. "Those windows won't stay shut. Something wants ta keep ya away from what is yers. Do ya understand?"

My brows pressed tight together. Fear swelled in my gut.

I don't understand.

"Listen carefully, Nora. Maybe somet'in' doesn't want ya findin' what's up there."

What will I find?

Landan let go of my wrist. "Anyway, I need ta be off. The fog is clearin'. You'll be a'right now."

He stood and wrapped his peacoat tighter around his middle.

I stared at him, awestruck, unable to process what he'd told me.

Landan grinned. That same unusual sparkle that gleaned from his eyes made my heart beat a little faster. "Glad I was here." He turned away. "And no more runnin' in the fog."

I stared after him with my mouth agape, until he was swallowed up by the fog.

Two faint, glowing circles closed in where Landan disappeared. I stood to my feet. The closer they came, the brighter they appeared, until they revealed themselves as the front headlights of Declan's car. He sailed in quickly, grinding to a sliding halt on the gravel.

He hopped out of his car. I stepped toward him. Pain spasmed from my knees. I hissed through my teeth as I limped forward.

Declan's mouth gaped. "What's happened to ya?" He lifted

my chin with his finger. "Yer bleedin'." He glanced down at my knees. "And you've torn through the knees of yer joggers."

I looked down. "Oh—I hadn't noticed."

His mouth hung wider, seemingly waiting for me to explain.

"I—I was running, and I couldn't see. I fell."

"Good Lord, Nora!"

"I know. It was stupid. What're you doing here? I thought you had classes."

"Right, well"—he paused—"my da phoned me."

I locked eyes with him.

"I'm—I'm really sorry about yer ma."

Emotions flooded into my eyes. Tears leaked down my cheeks—I couldn't stop them.

I didn't have to tell him.

He pulled me into his arms. The warmth of his chest against my cheek unlocked more tears. I grabbed the edges of his jacket. Why had comfort like this evaded me since my mom died? I didn't get it from my dad.

His lips brushed the top of my head, sending a comforting electricity through my limbs. His hot breath seeped through my beanie and into my hair. I gripped him even tighter.

"Come on," he said. "Let's get ya cleaned up."

10

Declan

Declan set a hot cup of tea in front of me. "Here," he said, handing me a warm, wet cloth. "For your chin."

I hissed, pressing it against the cut. "How bad is it?"

"Nice-sized split just underneath your chin. Probably needs ta be butterflied."

I cringed but nodded. Declan brushed the sides of his thighs, appearing unsure what to do next. I was this broken thing, sitting on the couch. Now that he knew I was grieving, he was no different than everyone else back in Chicago—treating me like I might fall apart at any moment.

I'd already been doing that, hadn't I? I didn't want to be like this. Not here and not in front of Declan.

He joined me on the couch. "Drink some of that tea. It'll help."

I didn't have the stomach for anything but went ahead and took a sip, then ventured to meet his gaze. "I'm . . . I'm sorry I didn't tell you."

He shrugged. "I understand."

"Do you?" I needed to know.

"Well, no. I don't understand what it's like ta lose my ma. But—I kind of get why ya wouldn't want everyone ta know." He tapped his fingers on his knees. "Now I know what that look in yer eye is. It's the same one ya had when yer gran passed." He leaned forward, resting his forearms on his legs and folding his hands together. "It makes sense why I've been feelin' the way I did back then."

I tilted my head. "How's that?"

"Like I need ta steal ya away from a storm."

I like that. If only . . .

It made me feel like less of a burden—maybe even wanted. The tea and Declan's words helped. I took another drink.

"Remember when yer gran died? Ya ran ta my house, and I found ya sittin' on my doorstep."

My brows furrowed as the memory kindled in my mind. "I forgot about that."

"Seems like then."

I nodded. I'd told him everything, and he'd agreed to hide away with me until the pain went away—or our parents found us.

It was time to tell him everything.

And maybe, just maybe, he'll hide away with me again.

"It was just a few weeks ago." I chewed my cheek before continuing. "I was at university in Oregon, and my dad had been trying to call me. I ignored him. I was busy with classes, and he didn't usually call. My mom was the one who did that. Sometimes"—I pushed down a rise of emotion—"I don't know how to talk to my dad."

I sighed. "Later, my phone rang again. It said my mom was calling, so I answered. But it was my dad's voice on the other end. I asked him where Mom was—and why he was calling on her phone.

"I should've known something was up—that something was wrong. But I didn't. I was just annoyed that my dad had called instead of my mom. Like I'd been tricked into answering." My insides squirmed to say the next part out loud. "Dad told me that Mom had gone to the hospital earlier that day, and—she didn't make it.

"I remember waiting for it all to be some type of sick joke. She'd been healthy—never smoked or drank. Hadn't even been sick as far as I knew. My mind refused to believe it. I was numb—there was just nothing. Not even on the plane to Chicago the next day."

Declan leaned closer. "What happened to her?"

"I guess she had a disease that affected her bone marrow. The worst part is"—my gut tightened—"it was treatable as long as you caught the early signs. Apparently, my dad was too busy to notice." I gritted my teeth. "Mom too, I guess."

"That's terrible." Declan rested his palm on my back.

"Did you know that's what my gran died of too?"

"What?" His eyes widened. "No."

I nodded. "I thought she'd died of a stroke. That's what I'd been told, anyways. I didn't know until Mom passed that it'd been the same thing. My dad said I wasn't ready for all the details when I was little. *Whatever.*"

"Nora—I'm so sorry."

"I know."

Everyone is always so sorry.

I forced a smile. "The funeral was last Thursday. That's when it became real."

"Only a week ago?"

"Yeah." I stared into my tea, rubbing the mug's rim with my thumb. The mug was white and plain. I peered over my shoulder at the kitchen. I wanted Gran's mug. It would be nice to feel like she was close right now.

"My dad said I should stay in Chicago for a while and take a break from school. I refused. I didn't want to be around him, or in our house without Mom." I huffed. "My dad and I fought all the way to the airport."

"Ya came here instead."

"I don't really know why. It was like I was on autopilot once

I was inside the airport. I think I wanted everything back the way it was. Or to pretend it was, anyways."

"It's not, though, is it? The way it was."

I stared into Declan's eyes, uncertainty churning in my gut. He looked worried about what I would say. "I—I don't know. My gran isn't here. Neither is my mom. This house isn't the one I remembered. At least not really. But at the same time, I'm glad I came. Even though—"

"Even though, what?"

I pulled the cloth away from my chin and stared at the blood. Landan may be right. Maybe I was cursed.

Auntie Nieve, Gran, then Mom—am I next?

Landan said I was safe, but I wasn't so sure.

Should I tell Declan?

I didn't want him to give me *that* look. I was already a mess; I didn't want him to think I was crazy too.

"What is it?" Declan asked.

"Um . . . I saw Landan."

"Landan?" He scrunched his face, removing his hand from my back. "When?"

"Just before you drove up. He was there." I pointed toward the cliffs.

Declan's expression shifted. His jaw clenched, and he leaned back against the couch. "What was *he* doin' here?"

I stiffened at his hard tone. "He was just passing through. We spoke for a moment, and then he went on."

"Did he not see the state of ya?"

I shrugged. "Sort of."

Declan rolled his eyes and glared toward the window. They used to be friends—I thought.

Why do I feel the need to apologize?

Landan hadn't done anything wrong. Maybe it would help if Declan knew what Landan had done.

"If Landan hadn't been there, I would have—"

"Would've what?" His eyes narrowed, and he sat up.

"It was foggy, and I was running—"

My face heated, and I pleaded with my eyes for Declan to understand.

"Nora, what happened?"

I set down my tea and covered my face with my hands. "I don't want you to think I am stupid."

"Just tell me—I promise, I won't t'ink yer stupid."

"I was upset, and I was running really fast, and—"

His eyebrows raised.

"I sort of, almost ran off the edge of the cliff."

"What?" He snapped to his feet. His fingers raked his hair as he marched toward the window as if to spy the cliff's edge.

"Landan caught me. He saw me and was there in time."

"Nora!" His eyes were wide and his mouth gaped.

"I wasn't paying attention."

He just stared at me.

"I won't run in the fog again." I dropped my eyes to my lap. My chin trembled as tears welled up in my eyes.

Declan rubbed his hand down his face, then, after a long sigh, he returned to my side and held out his hand. "Hey, it's a'right now, anyway. Let me get the emergency kit. Got some iodine, gauze, and plasters under the kitchen sink ta get ya squared away."

I took his hand and squeezed it. "Thanks, Declan. But you know what? I think I am going to take a shower first. But maybe get the kit for me, so I can put some Band-Aids on after."

I had quite the gouge in my left knee. The joint was a bit swollen too. But it didn't ache as bad after the warm shower. I prodded it while sitting wrapped in a towel on the edge of the toilet lid.

I am going to feel this one for a while.

I placed one of the larger Band-Aids over the red wound, careful to avoid the road rash surrounding it.

Not broken. That's a plus.

I kicked at the pile of clothes on the floor—upset I'd ripped holes in my joggers.

Those were my favorite track pants. Too bad Gran's not here to sew my clothes like she used to.

I tsked.

Expensive too.

I had scrapes on my elbows and forearms. Most didn't need Band-Aids.

The crow's cawing echoed in my mind, and I held my breath. My pulse raced.

Was that really the sluagh?

I clutched my heart, squeezing my eyes shut.

Are they going to come for me again?

I glanced toward the closed bathroom door.

Should I tell Declan? I'm not even sure he'd believe me. He might even phone my dad. Landan believes me. I need someone to help. But what could either of them do?

I couldn't wrap my mind around what Landan tried to tell me. I shook my head and pulled on a pair of black, wide-legged stretch-pants—something that wouldn't press against my knees. I slipped on one of my favorite oversized sweaters—cozy but cute—then wiped the steam off the mirror with my towel and examined the cut on my chin.

I smiled at my reflection, patting my dark curls into place, pleased that the rose color of the sweater brought out the flush in my cheeks and lips. My fingers brushed my collarbone. The sweater dipped around my neckline, bringing out my best features.

Will Declan like how I look?

I lifted my chin, hissing at the thick, red, horizontal split just beneath it.

This looks awful.

I fished through the white and blue med kit to find the strips. I slid one out of the wrapper, but struggled to place it just right. I'd managed to get blood on the sticky part of the strip and needed a new one. I snatched another strip and tried again.

"Ugh! Why is this so hard!" I grumbled. "Another strip wasted." I sighed, exasperated, then went to grab another and hesitated. "Forget it." I opened the bathroom door. "Dec, can you help me?"

"Em . . . uh, sure," he responded from the kitchen.

"I need help butterflying my chin."

"Oh, uh, okay."

I went back to look in the mirror. My chin bled from messing with it, so I held a piece of cotton against it.

Declan appeared in the doorway. He rocked back on his heels, as though tentative to come inside. "My ma phoned. Em . . . she and Della are comin' over in a little while. Hope that's okay?"

That sounds really nice.

I nodded and held a strip out to him. He lingered in the doorway, his gaze darting between the floor and the hallway like he needed an escape route.

I couldn't help but grin at his hesitation. "Hey," I coaxed, "it's not weird. I just need a hand."

"Course," he replied, clearing his throat. He flashed an awkward smile, then entered and took the strip from my hand. "My ma thought it would be nice for ya ta have some warm dinner. Della's goin' ta stay the night wit' ya."

"Really?" I wasn't used to being taken care of like this. I liked it. I was especially glad I wouldn't have to sleep alone after what I'd seen earlier.

I hope Della'll forgive me for spilling coffee all over the floor.

It was nice to have the distraction of a warm family around.

"I t'ink ya might need more than one of these t'ings." He grabbed a few more strips from the kit. "Carla's back in town. She might be droppin' by later too."

I bit my cheek. "Does she know?"

Declan nodded. "My da called Don this mornin'."

"How's your dad?" I asked, looking at the floor instead of his eyes.

Declan's mouth twisted. "He's pretty broken up. He's known Una for most of his life. Quite the hard hit. For Carla too, but she still wants ta see ya." He pulled the back off the first strip. "Now lift yer chin." His hands neared my chin, then he wavered.

"Are you afraid of blood?"

"No, no. Just don't want ta hurt ya."

"I'll be all right." I grinned.

Concentration narrowed his eyes and tightened his lips. "I, ah, don't do this sort of t'ing often."

I laughed. "You'll do a better job than me. Went through two of those dumb strips before I asked for help."

He chuckled. "Shhh! Stop movin'."

"Okay, okay." I lifted my chin and held still.

Declan's fingers pressed the split together. His eyes bounced between my eyes and chin. He ran his finger over the first strip, sealing it, then grabbed another. He stuck the second one on, then his gaze lifted to mine and remained.

Those eyes.

"There." His fingers strayed from my chin to my jawline.

The same warm feeling from the night before flooded my chest. A satisfying ache pulled strings inside my heart. I didn't want him to stop looking at me like that—as though I were a long-lost ship returned to shore. But there was more— apparent desire burned beneath the dark lashes that framed his green eyes. My cheeks heated as I spotted a hint of brown in his left iris.

He leaned closer. "Yer so pretty."

I might explode.

He'd never said anything like that to me before. And yet, hadn't he always said as much with those lingering gazes? I'd never taken notice of them until now. How had I missed them?

Declan shook his head and took a step back. "Anyway." His face flushed a deep red, and his arms swung at his sides until he'd backed out of the bathroom. He thumbed toward the kitchen. "I, ah . . . I got us a snack. Some, eh . . . ham, butter, and brown bread."

Just like Mom used to make us. He remembered.

My heart was still caught in my throat, and my words fumbled, "S-Sounds great."

"Right," he said, disappearing down the hall.

I rested my fingers on my chin—the last place Declan touched—then turned toward the mirror. I smiled. The rose in my cheeks was a deeper shade of pink. My heart fluttered a hopeful patter inside my chest. I took a deep breath.

Did that just happen?

I wasn't sure as I floated toward the bathroom doorway, eager to join him. I paused at the door, then peered down the hallway at the locked stairwell.

What is it the sluagh don't want me to find?

I crept toward the stairway door and brushed my fingers on the silver knob.

Maybe Declan will come with me?

The memory of the wind howling my name and the windows rattling tore through my thoughts, and I yanked my hand away. I preferred this new reality. One where Declan's eyes stole me away from my sorrows. I shook my head and headed toward the kitchen.

The sluagh can wait.

11

Nightmares

"You cheated!" Della chucked her red game piece at Declan's face. He held up a couch pillow just in time to deflect it.

"I didn't." Declan swept his hand over the Catan board, his sea of blue pieces declaring his victory. He leaned back with a satisfied grin and folded his hands behind his head.

I rolled my eyes. "You won on a technicality that I'm pretty sure isn't legal."

"Ugh," he groaned. "Yous are just sore losers."

Della glanced at her watch and slapped her forehead. "It isn't one in the mornin'? I need ta go ta bed, else I'll be knackered tomorrow."

"Thanks for staying the night, Della."

"Sure, no problem." She grinned, squeezing my arm. "Ya've been t'rough a lot, and I wouldn't want ta sleep here alone."

"I'm stayin', too," Declan said. "Just need some pillows and a blanket for the sofa." He patted the green vinyl beneath him.

"Sure, yer not!" Della scolded.

"Ya have ta leave before the sun even rises anyway, Della. Who will keep Nora company when the rest of the livin' are awake? Besides, you'll be sleepin' here. It'll be fine. I'll keep ta the front of the house."

"Well"—Della winked—"it isn't as though ya didn't sleep here last night, anyway."

Declan's face flushed and his eyes flared. "It wasn't like that."

I giggled at the delight in Della's face for having upset her brother. It was clear she liked to get under his skin. It was easy to rile him with the right ammunition.

I scooped up some game pieces and dropped them back into the box. "Evidence of your win—destroyed," I teased.

"Not true." He clutched his chest in mock outrage, gasping. "More like—destroyin' the evidence of yer loss under my flawless victory."

"Right." I chuckled. "Whatever you need to tell yourself. We both saw what happened, right, Della?"

"That's the story," Della confirmed, joining my laughter.

"Anyway"—I sighed—"I appreciate you both being here. It was creepy here last night."

"Did ya like seein' Carla?" Declan helped gather up the pieces.

"Yeah." I pushed the box closer to him. "She was really close to Mom. Still called her on and off while we were in Chicago. Having her here was like having someone around that understood—even when she didn't speak. My mom kept a picture of the two of them on our mantle. Seeing her almost made me feel like my mom was here in some small way. Though I'm glad she and your mom left a little early." I placed my hand on my belly and curled my lip. "I don't think I could have handled another helping of lasagna, but I hated to refuse your mom's offers."

Della burst out laughing. "My ma t'inks food heals everyt'ing. Suppose that's where I get my love for bakin'."

Della was the spitting image of Patty, with their shared rosy, round cheeks and bright brown eyes. The warm, delicious food and fellowship had certainly lifted my spirits.

I stood and stretched, trying not to notice Declan's lingering gaze. I put my arms down and nonchalantly straightened my clothes. "I'm going to go to bed."

"Me too." Della got up and gave me a hug.

Declan stood.

"Well . . . um? Goodnight," I said, lifting my arms to hug him just as he reached for me. I faltered, lowering my arms, unsure if I should go through with it, or if it was sort of . . . forced. I hugged him anyway.

"That wasn't awkward at all," Della snorted. "Yous two." She shook her head. "I'm goin' ta wash, then hittin' the pillow."

"Night," I called as she disappeared down the hall. I forced a sideways smile at Declan without fully meeting his eyes, then I was off. Embarrassment quickened my strides down the hallway to my grandparents' old room.

I swiped the heavy curtains closed, then jumped into bed, wrapping the turquoise duvet around me. The newer windows felt safer in this room. They weren't French windows like the ones upstairs, or at Don and Carla's. I kept my door open a crack. Light from the bathroom lit up the bedroom. Apparently, Della didn't like it dark either.

Della slept in the other bedroom, while Declan took the couch in the living room.

I'm glad he stayed.

Maybe his presence would keep the sluagh at bay. It had the night before.

I tossed and turned with thoughts of Declan and Landan crowding my head. The screeching crow infiltrated my peace, and I shoved my fingers into my ears as if that could silence the memory. I squeezed my eyes tight, willing myself to sleep.

I focused on Declan, and how I wished that he had kissed

me. I'd never thought of Declan that way before, but now I couldn't stop. I kept trying to capture his gaze during our game, but we never connected—at least not in any way that told me anything. Had I made the whole thing up? Telling me I was pretty didn't mean he liked me. Or did it?

"Ugh," I groaned as my insecurities pinged.

Just empty your mind.

An hour passed before the train of my thoughts blurred. A rhapsody of my anxious, half-conscious imaginations melded together, and I faded into a fitful sleep.

I woke with a start. Rain pounded the windowpane. Everything in the house was quiet—as it should be in the middle of the night—but something was different. Obscure.

It's storming hard out there.

Gusts of rain slammed against the house like waves smacking the siding. I kicked my feet, tossing and turning as nervousness riled my stomach. My thoughts went to Declan in the living room, and I rolled out of bed.

Maybe the storm woke him too.

I snuck toward the door. But something—a feeling— turned me back toward the window.

Thunder pealed, and I jumped. White lightning lit the edges of the curtain with pulsing light.

I need to look.

Something beckoned to me just outside the window. The hairs on my arms stood on end as I pulled the curtain back.

Lightning webbed the sky, revealing a man standing outside my window. I screamed, flinging the curtain closed. But an invisible hand flung both curtains wide open again. Fear crawled up my skin like tiny spiders. I lurched backward until the bedframe hit the back of my legs. My eyes widened as the darkly silhouetted man stared back at me.

He held out his hand. Something dangled from his wet fingers. Lightning burst again, highlighting the man's porcelain face. Dark, dripping-wet hair covered his eyes.

"Landan?" I cried. My heart beat faster than a raven's wings caught in a storm. I moved closer with slow, steady steps. Landan stood there like an ominous statue, holding out his hand. Rain flooded over him like a dark tide swallowing the shore.

"Landan," I called through the window. I needed him to respond, to say something, to keep the horror slithering beneath my skin from tearing its way out.

He moaned. His lips moved, but I couldn't understand him.

I pressed my hand against the ice-cold window. My breath fogged the glass.

His muffled voice groaned louder.

I leaned closer. A sharp chill brushed the back of my neck. My gran's rosary dripped between his fingers.

Landan cried louder, "N-O-R-A!"

A petrified scream tore from my gut. The raucous thunder stole its sound. Large black wings loomed behind Landan, lit by lightning.

I woke up clutching my chest.

It was only a dream.

But what kind of dream was that? I glanced at the window. No rain or storm. Early morning light filtered through the edges of the curtains. I exhaled in relief.

The image of Landan stole through my thoughts, reigniting my terror. In those final moments, he had become the villainous voice I had been running from. My breathing calmed, and the ebbing adrenaline released prickles of cold sweat on my brow.

What was Landan trying to tell me?

He'd sounded like the sluagh but held my gran's rosary.

It doesn't matter. It was just a dream. Probably all my anxious thoughts meshing into one big nightmare.

I rolled out of bed and crept toward the window. I lifted the curtain to the illuminating colors of an early morning sunrise. Clear skies. No fog. The iciness outside leaked through the windowpane.

I rubbed my arms and grabbed a sweatshirt from my suitcase. I pulled it on and opened my bedroom door, careful not to wake Declan. Della had already left. Her bedroom door was ajar, revealing a vacant bed.

I tiptoed to the living room. Declan had his arms tossed above his head. I cupped my hand over my mouth to stifle a giggle at his disheveled hair. One long leg drooped over the back of the sofa.

The keys to the upstairs sat on the coffee table. I peered over my shoulder at the hallway. Curiosity nipped at my thoughts.

What might be up there?

I scooped the keys from the table. Declan hadn't stirred—his deep breathing a sign I hadn't disturbed him.

My gran's rosary caught my eye. It lay on the floor just beneath the coffee table. The memory of the rosary's dark beads, dripping with rain between Landan's fingers, gave me pause before I clenched it into my fist.

Why the rosary? What did it all mean?

I glanced back to the hallway.

I hate to go up there by myself.

Declan's steady breath carried a peaceful rhythm. He was so handsome—even with the unflattering slack of sleep tugging his features into a wide-mouthed gape.

I'd rather stay here. What could there possibly be for me to find?

I sighed, releasing what was left of my reluctance.

Declan will be right here—only one scream away if I need him.

I stole down the hallway toward the stairs, slid the key into the door, and unlocked it.

Click.

I bit my lip and turned the knob. The door opened with a low groan. A rush of cold air blew past me. My stomach swirled.

Window must be open. Again.

My mind was already made up. My curiosity peaked.

Move. Landan said something was up there. Though, how could he know that?

It didn't matter. I was already on my way up the stairs. The floorboards creaked beneath my steps, so I quickened my pace to not prolong the racket any longer than necessary.

Now at the top, I faced my old bedroom. The door was ajar. The sheer white curtains flailed in the open window.

I swallowed—my hesitation returning. Dim, eerie light seeped into the room.

This is dumb.

I switched on the light.

I am closing those windows and searching those boxes.

I marched forward, my skin prickling as I crossed the bedroom. I grabbed the two windowpanes and latched them shut.

There.

I nodded, calming my heightened nerves.

"Meow."

I leapt into the air, muffling a scream with my hands. Buttons sat curled up on the bed, blinking at me.

"Buttons," I whispered. "If you startle me one more time, I'm going to toss you over the cliff."

The cat rolled its cheek against the quilt, as though beckoning me to pet him.

I let out a perturbed breath and folded my arms. "Was it you that pushed the window open?"

He curled his head into his paws and closed his eyes. A purr rumbled from his furry black rib cage. I couldn't resist sifting my hand through the soft fur of his underbelly.

"I wouldn't want to sleep outside either," I said, rubbing my fingers over his cheek. "I'll let you stay while I'm up here. But as soon as I am gone, you're out. You can earn your stay by being my guard. Keep the sluagh out. Can you do that for me?"

He lifted his head and gazed at me like he'd understood what I said.

"Right." I nodded. "Glad we are in agreement."

I sat down on the bed next to him and inspected my gran's rosary. Why had it been in my dream? I shrugged and wrapped it around my wrist. A rough pattern interrupting the cross's smooth finish captured my eye. I held it closer and ran my fingers over it. Along one side of the cross was a small inscription I'd never noticed before.

"Nieve Sheehy." I lifted my head. "Huh?"

This is Aunt Nieve's rosary?

12

Breadcrumbs

"Huh? That's strange."

Why did Gran have Nieve's rosary?

I finished wrapping the rosary around my wrist.

I don't understand why Landan had it either.

I fingered a bead. The rosary had something to tell me. A history that'd been buried.

What am I meant to know?

I glanced at Buttons as if he could answer the thoughts swirling in my head, then scanned the room full of boxes. More boxes awaited in the other room down the hall. The sheer weight of the task loomed over me.

"Ugh." I smirked.

Guess I should get to work.

I moved to stand, but my foot nudged something on the floor—the book of fairy tales Declan had been looking at the other day. He'd abandoned it when we ran for our lives. I shot a suspicious glance at the windows, then down at the cat.

"Still got my back, buddy?"

He didn't move.

"I'll take your silence as a yes. If you're not worried, not sure why I should be."

I chuckled, then picked the book up off the floor. It had landed face down with the pages open. I turned it over and flattened the bent pages with my palm. The pages were still open to Hansel and Gretel. The faint colors detailed Hansel leaving a breadcrumb trail so he and Gretal could find their way home. Nefarious black birds watched from tree limbs, as though waiting to eat them up. Their cawing reverberated inside my mind.

I shuddered and closed the book. Birds had become the demons of my nightmares. I set the book on the bed, then inspected the first tower of boxes. The pile was three medium boxes high. I pulled open the folded cardboard panels. Inside were items wrapped in white packing paper. I pulled out the first object and unwrapped it, revealing one of Gran's animal figurines.

I smiled. She'd owned a collection of colorful woodland animals, each holding a different instrument, which she used to display along the mantelpiece. This one was a red fox in a green checkered vest, playing a violin.

This whole box is probably her figurines.

I set the box down and was about to open the next one when footsteps creaked up the stairs. Declan's head poked through the doorway.

"Good mornin'." He grinned, holding a steaming mug in each hand. "Hope I'm not botherin' ya."

"Of course not. Glad you're awake. Hate being up here by myself."

"It was a bit spooky the other day." He approached with a steady stride so as to not spill the mugs.

"You're always bringing me tea."

"How do ya know these aren't both for me?" Declan feigned taking a sip from both. "Ah now, it's the Irish t'ing ta do now, isn't it? The world stops turnin' wit'out a proper cuppa. The kettle wasn't warm, so I knew ya hadn't had one." Declan shuddered. "Freezin' up here."

I pointed to the cat lying on the bed. "The window was wide open. I think Buttons was the culprit."

Declan chuckled. "Awe, now I see you weren't alone." He tsked. "That daft lil' cat. Always up causin' problems wit' that window." Declan handed me my tea in Gran's mug. I cupped it in my hands like a treasure. "Me ma did the dishes yesterday. T'ought ya might like ta have that one."

"Thanks," I said, meeting his gaze. A glimmer of longing lingered in his eyes. My cheeks warmed like the mug in my hands. Where had his glances been the evening before? Maybe he wanted to keep Della at bay. I couldn't say I blamed him.

He broke eye contact and scanned the room. "Decided ta brave the boxes, huh?"

"Yeah, well"—I sighed, pressing my lips together—"I had a strange dream last night that made me curious. Yesterday when I saw . . ." I stopped, not wanting to mention Landan again.

"Saw what?"

What do I say?

Declan lowered his gaze to meet mine. "Is everyt'ing a'right? Was it a bad dream?"

"Sort of."

"Do ya want ta talk about it?" Declan asked, walking over to the bed and taking a seat next to Buttons. He scratched the cat underneath its chin.

"I told Buttons he could stay as long as he kept the sluagh out."

Declan's hand froze mid-scratch, and he faced me with a sideways smirk. "Nora."

My heart sank. I wanted to tell Declan everything, but he wouldn't believe me. Was it worth risking him thinking I'd lost my mind? Maybe he'd leave, or worse. "It . . . it was just a dream."

I looked away and settled on the floor. I sipped my tea, swallowing down the swell of grief tightening in my throat. I needed Declan to be with me in this. If he couldn't help, then Landan—

"Did I upset ya?"

"I, um—" I glanced at the window. Peaceful, newly risen sunlight streamed through the curtains.

"Forgive me." He scooted off the bed and joined me on the floor. He leaned forward, capturing my eyes. "Truly. Tell me about yer dream . . . th-the sluagh. All of it."

There's nothing to fear in telling him my dream. It's not like I was conscious for any of it.

"There was a thunderstorm. It was raining hard. Out the window was a dark man holding my gran's rosary. It was so—scary." I set my mug on the floor and unwrapped the rosary from my wrist. I held it toward Declan. He pulled it from my fingers. "This morning, I found something on it." I pointed. "Look at the side of the cross."

He lifted it to his eyes.

"Just underneath the bottom edge there."

He squinted as he read. An obvious understanding lit his face. "This was yer aunt's?"

"Yeah." I nodded. "I wonder why my gran had *her* rosary? Perhaps to keep a piece of Nieve with her." I peered over my shoulder at the boxes. "I've been wanting to go through these boxes anyway, but now—"

"Now yer hopin' ta find somet'ing more about yer family."

"Maybe." I shrugged. "Not really sure what it is I'm looking for. But, there might be something. I figure I'll know once I find it."

Declan pressed his lips together. His eyes softened. "Let me help ya look. Especially wit' Buttons keepin' guard for us, we have quite the opportunity. Right, Buttons?" He stood and patted the cat. "No scary wind can chase us back down those stairs as long as yer here."

The cat's pur increased as Declan's attention seemed to mean he might get more pets.

My heaviness lifted. Declan's words always had a soothing effect on me. "Do you have the day free?"

"Well"—he approached a stack of boxes—"not goin' ta my classes today. It's a light load on Fridays, anyway. But I do have ta help my da wit' a few t'ings at the shop later. You could come wit' me and hang wit' Della. She'd like that, and it's better than hangin' out here all alone. I have the mornin' free, though." He opened the lid of the first box and chortled. "We won't be finding much in this box." He pulled out a long, teal satin nightgown, dangled it back and forth, and wiggled his brows. "Looks like a box of clothes."

"Yeah, that's my gran's nightgown." I smiled. "I used to put on that gown and pretend I was a princess." I giggled. "Silky nightgowns were perfect for imaginary ballroom dances."

Declan pressed his hand against his chest, sarcasm apparent in his offended gape. "And yet, I was never invited ta even one of yer grand affairs." He winked.

"No room for boys in my make-believing, apparently."

He tsked, folding his arms. "Well, ya missed out. Plenty of top-tier super hero adventures happenin' up here." He tapped his temple. "Would've brought some real excitement ta yer fancy parties."

"You're right. Totally missed out." I laughed. "Anyway, two boxes down." I rose to my feet to filter through the next box in my pile. "Declan?"

"Yah?"

I fiddled with the lid of the box in front of me. "I can't help but feel like I have disrupted everything in your life since I came here."

Declan paused and turned my way. "Nora"—he exhaled, rubbing the back of his neck—"I've been waitin' for ya ta disrupt my life since the day ya left."

I couldn't stop a smile from curling my lips. "Good," I said, a good deal of heat pulsing into my ears.

"Good," he replied, opening the next box. "Let's get ta work, then."

"Ugh," Declan groaned, arching his back into a long stretch. "I'm about done."

"Yeah, me too." It'd been tedious but rewarding to go through all the boxes. We still had a whole other room to go, but I loved that we'd searched most of the ones in this room. I had a growing pile of treasures on the bed next to Buttons. He was busy attacking a necklace that must have looked a little too much like a tempting insect.

"Buttons." I giggled, rescuing the necklace from his grasp, then returned to my last box. "This box is just a bunch of my grandad's Readers' Digests. Not sure why your mom boxed some of these things up." I huffed with a weary smile. "Could've just been thrown away."

"Ya never know what's goin' ta be sentimental."

"True. Not going to even bother looking through this box, though." I pulled a magazine from the top of the box and thumbed through it. A puff of dust wafted into the air. I waved it away with a cough. "These have definitely been here a while."

A surge of sadness pricked my heart. Mom would never go through these boxes. Anything that might've held any sentimental value stopped with me. My dad wouldn't want any of it. "No one else will be opening these boxes. Just me."

I slapped the magazine back in the box, pressing my hand against my forehead. "I mean, now that I'm here"—my voice trembled—"we can get rid of most of these things. I could—I could hire someone to come pick up the boxes and take them to charity, or-or the dump."

Declan approached and smoothed his hand over my back. The warmth of his touch unlocked a tear. "I don't t'ink ya need ta make any of those decisions just yet."

I nodded, thankful for the reminder. Sniffing, I wiped my eye and let out a soft chortle. "I'm hungry. And my tea is cold."

Declan laughed. "Time for lunch, then."

"Definitely."

"We can clean this mess up later."

"We?" I grinned at him. "You know you don't have to help me do all of this."

"Ah." He tsked. "Come on now. Don't stop a man offerin' ta help."

I held up my hands in defeat. "Fine. I won't." I stood and my knee accidentally knocked the box over. Readers' Digests spilled out across the floor, along with a load of old notebooks and what looked like a few journals. "What are these?" I bent down and riffled through the notebooks. Declan joined me on his knees and picked one up.

Ripped and crinkled pages filled the spiral-bound notebooks. My gran's handwriting scratched the pages. I swiped through, finding scattered thoughts, notes, and shopping lists. One page held a recipe, another directions.

After thumbing through three notebooks, I reached for a journal—a basic black, faux leather hardback. No other details except a ribbon that bookmarked the pages. I opened the cover and gasped as I read the first page:

This Journal belongs to: James Morrigan.

Declan leaned over. "It's yer da's!"

My wide eyes lingered on the page as my fingers traced the deep grooves left by the pen. Their path ended at the black ribbon hanging out from the bottom. My jaw locked. Anger percolated in my gut.

What do I care what my dad had to say?

I turned to the bookmarked page regardless.

September 25th, 2013

Declan commented, "Just a little over ten years ago."

My nerves tingled as my fingers clenched the pages, as if eager to crunch them with my fists. They might hold possible answers, but—no. I slammed the book shut.

Declan jumped. "Don't ya want ta read it?"

Of course I want to read it. But why did it have to be Dad's? Why couldn't it have been Mom's journal?

My thoughts drifted to my cell phone downstairs. I'd happily ignored its pings for several days now. I'd eventually have to check those messages, though. Most would be from Dad. "I am just—not sure I want to. Maybe later."

"Course." Declan gathered up the other two journals in the pile. "These ones later too?"

I nodded again, but then raised my hand. "Wait. Can you tell me who those journals belong to?" I side-eyed the thin hardbacks, covered with old stained fabric. One was orange, the other a light blue. Declan opened the orange one.

His brows scrunched. "It doesn't have a name."

I leaned closer.

Gran's handwriting.

I snatched it from his hands. The date of the first page was 19th October, 1964.

"Wow!" I said, snatching the other one. My gran's same handwriting was all over the pages in that journal too. "This one is a little later—1966. My gran would have been"—I did the math in my head—"nineteen." I couldn't wait to sink my teeth into *these* journals. "This is what I was looking for."

"Do you want me ta leave ya ta look t'rough them?"

I studied the journals in my hands. "No. Later. I really am hungry. If I start looking at them now—I know myself—I won't be able to stop. Maybe I can read them while I'm at Della's."

"Grand." Declan rose to his feet. I tried not to notice that he'd picked up my dad's journal to take with him. My instinct was to surrender it back to the pile of Readers' Digests and never look back.

That's probably why he grabbed it.

Declan had a determined look in his eye as he shoved it beneath his arm, a look that said he was rescuing it from the bins.

I didn't care anymore. I had Gran's journals.

Maybe they'll tell me something, maybe they won't. Either way, I can't wait to read them.

13

Gran's Journals

"What ya got there?" Della asked as Declan disappeared into the post office.

"I found these journals that belonged to my gran. Declan and I went through some of the boxes upstairs this morning, and—"

Della's implicating grin and chortle halted my story.

"That's all we were doing, Della. Going through old boxes."

"Is that what they're callin' it now? My friends and I just call it snoggin'."

I smirked, putting my hands on my hips. "We weren't kissing. If we were, I wouldn't have found these." I held up the journals. "That's not to say I wouldn't like to know what Declan's thinking."

Della chuckled. "Come on! Don't tell me ya don't know. Even I know what he's thinkin'."

"Oh, yeah?" I rolled my eyes and crossed my arms. "All I know is that he's forever been my best friend. Ever since I came back—it's like we picked up right where we left off. I am glad for that. Especially after all our time apart. But other than maybe a few stray glances, I am not sure there is anything more to report."

Della's eyes glittered. "So ya like him, then?"

"No." I gasped. "I mean—" Which words did I need to

shovel back into my mouth? "I'm just saying that he hasn't given me a strong indication of his feelings. At least"—I peered toward the post office—"not really."

He did call me pretty. He's been at my beck and call. He's said things like he'd been waiting for me to come back.

Other than knowing I never wanted him to leave, I didn't know how to feel about Declan. And—I really wish he'd kissed me. I hadn't expected any of this when I booked my flight. Or had I?

Declan appearing from behind those boxes three days ago flashed through my mind. It was like an avalanche of pent-up longing tumbled off my shoulders. He was back in my life—after all these years—*him*. All I wanted to see was him.

What had I been aching for all these years? Why *did* I come back?

Della called me back from my thoughts. "I don't mean ta slag ya. Love seeing my brother turn red. But, I *do* know what he t'inks about ya. That's why I love harassin' him. He's never stopped talkin' about ya. Never stopped hurtin' about that day ya left."

"Yeah." My face fell. "I hated that day too. It's haunted me for years. Even now that I'm back—I'm still so angry at my dad for not letting me say goodbye."

"Hey." Della touched my arm that hugged the journals to my chest. "I'm sorry for dredging up that day. Ya want somet'ing ta drink?"

"Love a latte. Maybe I can keep from spilling it all over your floor this time. Sorry about that, by the way."

Della tsked. "Stop that. I don't t'ink a single one of us are blamin' ya for that." She peeked over her shoulder. "Da hasn't really been the same since the news. I wished I could've known yer ma. The way my parents talk about her—she must have been a great friend."

"You don't remember her at all?"

"Oh, I do—a little. But not'in' really sticks out. I remember you, yer ma, and da being around. Kind of just there in the background of my early memories. But I don't remember details." She turned away to start making my drink.

I held up the journals. "You mind if I sit and read these for a while."

"Course not. Let me get ya yer coffee." The espresso machine hissed as she went to work. A rich blend of roasted coffee beans with notes of vanilla floated to my nose. "Want anyt'ing else? Another sausage roll?"

"Nah. Just the coffee's fine. Declan and I ate before we came."

She set my cup down in front of me, shaking her head with a smirk. "Ya know how ridiculous ya are?"

"What?"

"Are ya really wonderin' if my brother likes ya? Come on now, gurl."

"Not this again." I giggled, bringing the cup to my lips. "Mmmm! Yum."

She curtsied with an of-course-it's-perfect sort of smile. "Only the best."

"If your brother wants me to know something—he'll tell me." I walked to the table by the window.

"Wit' the two of yous actin' like this, we'll never get anywhere."

I waved her off and settled into my chair, a grin tugging at my lips. I had almost as much fun bantering with her as I did Declan.

She gave me a cheeky eye roll, then returned to her work. I picked up the first journal—the orange one from 1964. I took a nice full sip of my coffee, then opened to the first page:

19th October, 1964

Sister Bridget says we've ta start keepin' journals now—like a sort of confession, she calls it. Says it'll be good for us. I don't see the point, but here I am, scribblin' away. What's there ta say, really? I'm just another girl at St. Margaret's, an all-girls Catholic school, same as nearly every other Irish girl I know.

If this is meant ta be a log of my life, well, here's the truth: Me mam's dead, God rest her soul. Me da's a useless drunk. And me? I've been snoggin' Finn James behind O'Malley's bakery after school, smokin' a fag or two for good measure.

I gasped, bringing my hands to my lips. The thought of my gran being so scandalous had me at a loss for words.

Wouldn't it be grand ta see the look on Da's face if he ever found out? Not that he would. He's barely home—out workin' by day and drinkin' wit' the lads by night.

I hate him. I truly do. Sometimes I wish he'd just drink himself right off the cliffs and be done wit' it. All he's good for is tetherin' us to this house, the same one where Mam died. He's t'reatened ta take me out of school more than once, says I should be at home "cleanin'" and "lookin'" after t'ings." But Auntie Nils won't hear any of it. She's the only one standin' between me and a life of misery in this place.

Poor Nieve. She's scared stiff of bein' in the house on her own. Says she hears t'ings—whispers, creaks, and shadows movin' when they shouldn't. Can't say I blame her. She spends most of her time at Auntie Nils's anyway. She's two years younger, and not yet ready for secondary school, but I'll make sure she's never stuck in the town once she's old enough.

One more year till me exams. After that, I'm takin' Nieve and we're leavin' this place for good.

I looked up. Apparently, all the men in our family were slouches.

Well . . . I guess my dad isn't a slouch. Absent—definitely. Don't really want him to be involved in my life, though. He already ruined it.

My grandad was fine, but I hadn't really known him. He was just there, like a silent fixture in the house. Probably why I wasn't all that sad when he passed. Gran had said it was the military that ruined him. That was my great-grandad's excuse as well. Though at least he had World War II to blame for that. Not sure what my grandad's reason was. No one ever said.

Gran had grown up in The Flaherty House. Named after my grandad, but the original house belonged to her father, Patrick Joseph Sheehy. It was strange to read in her journal that she wanted to leave. She always seemed to love this place when I was a child.

It's interesting that her mother also died when she was young. I didn't know that before. And Auntie Nieve was afraid of the house.

I dove back in but found most of the pages lined with talk about the boy she liked to kiss and complaints about the maths she struggled with at school. I scanned a little more, hoping to find any important nuggets. Months leapt between entries when my eyes finally landed on something intriguing:

25*th* June, 1965

Da's finally stopped yammerin' on about me quittin' school. Only one year left now, and I suppose he knows there's no point fightin' me anymore. I've always been the strong-willed one— he was never winnin' that battle. But now he's turnin' his eye to Nieve, and it makes me blood boil.

She's startin' secondary school after the summer, and wit' Auntie Nils not as involved these days, Da's got a stronger grip on t'ings. His heavy hand's harder ta push against now. He's already talkin' about pullin' her out ta work at the seamstress's shop. It's not right—she's only fourteen, just about ta turn fifteen. She should be laughin' wit' her friends and learnin' about the world, not chained ta some sewing machine.

He'll ruin her life, just like he's tried ta ruin mine.

Something in my chest tightened as I read that line. I'd said those very words before. My dad took away my choice, and that was why I'd been happy to put distance between us at university.

I've been workin' part-time at the supply shop with Mr. Patterson.

Mr. Patterson. I bet that's Declan's great-grandad's shop!

Da takes every penny I earn and spends it wherever he's drinkin' these days. If it weren't for the groceries and clothes Auntie Nils helps wit' now and then, we'd have nothin'. But wit' her pullin' back, wit' us bein' older, and a new husband to boot, I'm worried sick. I've been hidin' bits of money here and there, stuffin' it where Da won't find it.

Nieve's found herself a friend—a boy, though his name escapes me. He keeps her company, and she seems ta like him well enough. I'll need ta keep an eye on that. Can't have her followin' my path, sneakin' 'round wit' lads behind bakery walls. She deserves better than that.

Still, if t'ings get worse, I'm ready ta run. Once I've saved enough, I'll take her away from this place, Da be damned. She'll have a proper chance at a life, one he'd never give her.

That was it—the end of the orange journal. I closed the book and rested my chin on my palm. Other customers had filtered in and out, and Della took an order from a couple at the counter.

I stared out the window in deep thought. The journal

stirred my curiosity about Aunt Nieve. Gran's and her life had clearly been more dire than mine, yet certain aspects deeply resonated with me, connecting me to this aunt I'd never met.

"Hey!" Declan's voice pulled me out of my contemplation.

I smiled at him before lifting my coffee for another sip. Empty. I tsked, gazing at the light brown lines left behind.

"You seemed lost in t'ought." He floated over and settled in the chair across from me. "Journals givin' ya a lot ta t'ink on?"

"Definitely." I grinned. "Finished this one already." I patted my hand on the orange journal. "There wasn't a whole lot of interest in there, except that my gran liked to kiss some boy behind a bakery."

"No." Declan gasped.

"Yeah. Smoking too."

"Shockin'!" He grinned, leaning forward, as though eager for more.

"I know, right?" I giggled. "Though I guess the smoking part isn't that outlandish. I mean, it was the sixties, and she obviously developed—and kept—the habit. There were some other interesting bits, though. Apparently, my great-gran died in The Flaherty House, and my great-grandad was a drunk. He made it really difficult for my gran and Aunt Nieve."

"Ya didn't know that before?"

"Nope. Was news to me. I mean . . . I knew that my gran grew up in that house, but I didn't know some of those other things. My mom didn't tell me a lot about Gran. And my gran probably didn't want to divulge all her dark secrets when I was little. Anyway"—I sighed—"are you done?"

He grimaced. "Not quite yet. I should've been, but my da is a little out of sorts today."

I nodded.

I know the feeling.

"He asked me ta do a few extra t'ings. Ya still don't mind hangin' out here?"

I shook my head. "I could go for another coffee. And I still have this whole other journal to get through. Luckily, they aren't very long. My gran's handwriting is so big. Took her several pages to not say a whole lot."

"Grand." He pressed his palms against the table, moving to stand, then halted. "I—I wanted to ask ya somethin'." He peered over at Della, then turned back to meet my curious gaze.

"Yeah?"

"Em—" Declan glanced down at his hands. "I thought maybe later, you and I could get somethin' ta eat together."

"Go to Don's and get some chips, or something?"

"No." His face flushed at my remark. His feet pointed toward the door as though ready to retreat. "I mean, like—like somewhere nice. Like the Wharf—like a date."

The empty cup slipped from my hands, clattering against the table as I scrambled to catch it.

Declan straightened and took a step back. "I mean . . . only if ya wanted ta. We don't have—"

"Yes."

His eyes widened, and a sheepish grin curled one side of his mouth.

Giddiness swept over me, like a teenage girl whose crush just asked her to the prom. My clumsy words tumbled out from my mouth. "I'd love—I mean, I, uh—want to go." I set my elbows on the table, trying to play it cool, and cupped my hands over my blushing cheeks.

This is so stupid. This is Declan. Why am I so flustered?

I peeked over to the counter. Della stood there, grinning from ear to ear. She hadn't missed it.

Dang it.

14

The Cave

"**G**rand," Declain said, bounding back toward the post office. "Another hour or two. Then I'll come get ya. It's a date."

"Yeah, a date," I called back, trying not to swallow my tongue. I buried my head in the journal and peered over the pages at Della.

Declan stopped at the entryway and pointed at her. "Not a word from ya."

She twisted her fingers over her lips like she'd locked her lips with a key. Her beaming smile said it all, though. Declan shook his head and disappeared around the corner. Before turning back to her work, she mouthed, "See—I told ya."

My head spun. I couldn't focus on the blue journal. My insides bounced like a raging party. I closed my eyes, rubbed my temples, and exhaled a deep sigh.

Calm down.

The urge to dart over to Della and spill everything tugged at me, but the steady stream of customers anchored me in place. I had no choice but to get a grip without her help.

I rolled my eyes and opened Gran's second journal. I flipped through the first two pages. My eyes read the date *19ᵗʰ August, 1966,* but I couldn't focus on much else. My mind was a swirl of Declan's green eyes, and him telling me he'd been waiting for me to disrupt his life since the day I'd left. My insides squealed.

I flipped through page after page, my heart beating to a joyful rhythm I couldn't quiet. Boys had asked me out before, but none had ever made my heart flutter like this. This was Declan. He was different—special.

I know it. I've always known it.

My fingers kept turning the pages, until I landed on *23rd September, 1966.*

That's the date Mom died. September 23rd, 2024.

I stared at the page, tracing the spots where the blue pen ink had bled from water soaking the paper.

Or, are they tears? Too few to be rain or water damage.

Declan faded to the back of my mind. I leaned closer to the page.

23rd September, 1966

I tried to protect her. God help me, I tried. But the Garda found her this mornin'. Nieve's gone. She drowned in that awful cave.

My eyes widened and my mouth hung open. Aunt Nieve drowned in the cave—*the cave.* My memory swirled with the black water and Declan's hand losing me to the salty abyss.

I can barely write the words. My hands are shakin', and my eyes won't stop spillin'. Nieve—my sweet lil' sister. Only sixteen. Too young for all this. Too young ta understand what she was caught up in.

That boy—that boy—he filled her head wit' ideas. Foolish notions of prayer and forgiveness, as if either would save her from Da. If she'd listened ta him much longer, he'd have had her runnin' off ta a nunnery. <u>Time doesn't heal!</u> Not for me, and it sure didn't for her.

And that boy . . . there's somethin' not right about him. I swear it. He's like Lucifer in sheep's clothes. I've seen it—a shadow in his eyes, like somet'ing ancient and unrighteous is hidin' behind that beautiful face of his. If I didn't know better, I'd say he's one of them shifters—the daoine maithe. He fooled her, he did. Fooled her wit' his soft voice and promises. I got rid of him, but the others, they're harder ta chase away.

It was the voices. Nieve heard them—whispers in the wind, callin' her name. It all started wit' Mam—because of what she did. I've heard them too. I know now it's Balor. He's vengeful. He's been after us all this time, hasn't he? Between him, Da, and the sluagh, what chance did we ever have?

Da found some of the money last week. He was in a rage— tearin' t'rough the house like a storm. If he'd found all of it, we'd have no hope of gettin' away. So I told Nieve ta take what was left and hide it. I t'ought she'd go ta Auntie Nils's or ta the woods. I never t'ought she'd go ta the cave.

This is my fault. All of it. I sent her out. I didn't stop the curse. I should've kept her close, but I didn't. And now she's gone.

I clutched my stomach.
What did Great-Gran do?
The words on the page made me nauseous. How had Great-Gran cursed them? Cursed . . . us? Why did any of this have to have happened? The tragedy was near to my own skin. The voice of the sluagh now called my name.
What is this death that has leached onto my family?
Dread pulled me to my feet. Della's brows knitted and she tilted her head, looking at me like I had lost it. Could she sense it? Horror drained my blood as if Aunt Nieve's ghost stood in front of me.
It wasn't the sluagh that took Aunt Nieve—it was the cave. But wasn't it the sluagh that drove me to the edge of that cliff?

Panic. Pure panic buzzed through me, numbing my hands. The icy cold fingers of death had reached from the pages and clawed marks into my soul.

Della approached me, wiping her hands on a white towel. Maybe she could rescue me. Keep me from falling into the cursed arms of my family. She lifted her hand toward me. "Are ya all right, Nora?"

I tried to reply, but my throat locked.

Della's eyes lifted beyond me to the window. "Who's that?"

I spun around. He stood with his hands deep in the pockets of his peacoat. His dark hair gently blew over his eyes. "It—it's Landan."

"Who's Landan?" Della asked.

I didn't answer. My feet moved, and I pushed through the door, leaving Della and the journals behind.

Landan's narrowed eyes seemed to say he expected me.

"I need to go to the cave."

He nodded without a moment's hesitation. "Let's go."

I followed behind his long strides. The pace was quick, but I was a runner; I could keep up.

He spoke over his shoulder. "The tide should be low. It will be safe."

I scrunched my face.

Why do I want to go to the cave? To see it one more time?

"Landan?"

"Yah?"

"Why were you at Della's just now?" I asked, as we reached the end of the sidewalk and descended toward the lot that led to the shore.

"I was in town. Saw you in the window." He was quiet for a moment, then said, "Ya seemed distressed."

"I just read something in my gran's journal. You're right. There was a curse."

Landan stopped. I caught up to him and looked him in the

eye. A world of mysterious wisdom floated in his irises. He was part of this somehow. Here just when I needed him. Always.

"There is somet'in' that can be done about that, Nora. Ya need ta let some t'ings go."

"How do you know all this?"

His bright green eyes scanned my face. "Family has been here a while. Jus' like most of the ot'ers who've stuck around."

"How'd you know I wanted to go to the cave."

"I didn't. Ya told me that yerself. I didn't ask questions. Seemed ya needed help."

That makes sense.

"My Aunt Nieve drowned there." My spirit weighed heavy as I drew my gaze toward the cave.

He nodded and started walking again.

"You knew that?" I skipped to keep his pace.

"Yah."

My eyes widened. "How did you know and I didn't?"

"Suppose I pay attention."

That answer irked me, but I let it go. The cool breeze picked up from the shore, calming my nerves.

"What're ya hopin' ta find?" Landan asked, breaking the silence.

I chewed the inside of my cheek. "I guess I just need to see it again. I haven't been there since I also almost drowned. Honestly, I'm still not sure how I survived. Declan either."

"Got a guardian angel."

"Maybe." I shrugged—not in the mood for an ethereal hope.

We climbed down a sandy, pebbled trail. Swaying grass rose tall on both sides until the shale rocks broke the path. We turned left on the shore. In the gray distance, the rocky bluff where the cave hid spilled out into the sea. Over my shoulder, The Flaherty House was a white speck above the high cliffs on the other side.

I'd left my jacket behind at Della's. The wind on the beach bit through the fabric of my sweatshirt. I wrapped my arms around my middle to trap the warmth. It was almost a ten-minute trek before we reached the rocky lip.

"We won't have long," Landan said. His strides were quick, his eyes darting between the shoreline to the cave.

My cold cheeks were stiff. "The tide is coming in?"

"No, we have a bit more time before that happens, but the sun won't last. I don't have a torch ta light the cave. Do you?"

I puffed. "Of course I don't have a flashlight."

"Well, the natural light is all we have then. Let's go." He held out his hand and hoisted me up onto the three-foot rock. My knee ached as I climbed up—a reminder from my fall the day before. We lurched over the porous rocks, leaping across tide pools and breaks between boulders. The rock dipped down and the mouth of the cave came into view. The opening yawned eight feet high, like a giant banshee crying out, reminding me of the sluagh. My name whispered past my ears. I stepped back.

"It's all right," Landan said. "Yer safe."

"How can you possibly know that?" I glared at the cave, half-expecting the black crows that had chased me to swarm out from its dark opening.

"I'm not going ta force ya in, Nora. Yer the one that wanted ta come here."

"That's true. You're right. Okay." I swallowed my apprehension and stepped into the black. My eyes adjusted to the dull light as I climbed deeper inside. The cave was one long chamber, shaped like an L. Darkness shrouded the curving end of the cave. An angry pool swirled through a hole in the bottom. A broken path led along the side.

Nerves swelled, tightening my muscles as I stared at the swells below. The height dizzied my head. Even imagining a small stone plunging into the churning waves twenty feet below sent a visceral jolt of fear through me. I leaned back against the cave wall, craving stability.

"I can't believe Declan and I came in here as kids." I sighed in disbelief, fingers clutching at my chest. "What were we thinking? So dangerous."

"Don't know what it is about caves," Landan said, his voice echoing throughout the chamber, "but curious people have always been lured inside like rabbits inta a trap."

Landan's words heightened my caution. My adrenaline spiked.

What?

"Why would you say that?" I hollered, glaring at him.

His eyes were intense. "It's true."

The musty odor, mixed with the ocean's salty brine, soured my stomach. An eerie, hollow whistle blew through the cave. Spray from the water below hovered in the air. I took a step and my foot slipped, but I caught myself against the wall.

"Careful!" Landan grabbed my waist. "The algae is slippery."

"Thanks." I took a quick, steadying breath. "This is probably far enough."

"Right." Landan nodded. "No need ta go further." But his eyes halted on something. I followed his line of sight.

"What's that?" I pointed at something sitting on a raised ledge. It matched the rock but had more of an angular shape.

I need to see what that is.

That meant going deeper in. "I want to check it out."

"I t'ink it might be too high ta reach. It's not a good idea, Nora. Not in this light."

I looked him up and down. "Well, your height ought to do it."

"Maybe. How about ya let me go, then?"

"I'm the one that made us come here. I'm nimble. I'll be careful. We can do it together." My feet ambled along the narrow track toward the object. The rust color of what appeared to be a box stood out from the rockface.

"Careful, now!" Landan warned from behind. "Go slow."

"It's getting darker." My conscience pulled my eye toward the opening as though to a safe haven. The rebel in me bolstered and I tightened my lips, refusing to heed Landan's caution.

"Sun's going down. But ya still need ta take yer time. Not worth a fall."

"I know, I know," I agreed, my eyes on the prize. The closer I got, the more my heart raced. The object perched just above me. I reached for it, rising onto my toes.

"Just wait, Nora. I'm almost to ya."

So close.

"I've almost got it." My fingers brushed the edges of the tin as I balanced on one toe.

"Nora, just wait."

My foot slipped, and the narrow path was too steep to stop my momentum. My toes slid over the side.

Landan grabbed my wrist. "Got ya." He yanked me back to my feet. "Damn, gurl! That's two times I've saved ya from a ledge." He spun me to face him, his jaw tight, teeth bared. His furious tone cut through me like a sharp blade. "Could ya not have just waited? Ya just had ta have it, didn't ya? Don't ya ever t'ink that ot'ers might be affected by yer rash choices?"

My breath caught.

Dad said the same thing on the way to the airport.

Landan kept hold of me and reached for the box. His fingers strained until it scooted onto his palm. "Got it. Now let's get out of here."

I stood stock-still. Everything collided in my mind. I almost fell, and Landan's words stung. We climbed our way back out of the cave.

Why did I need that box so much?

The fresh air sifted through my hair.

I'm so glad to be out of there.

Landan exited behind me, his jaw still locked tight. A heated fire burned in his eyes.

"Here's yer damned box." He dropped it into my hands.

It was heavier than I'd anticipated, and I almost dropped it. The box was a rusted metallic container. Portions of the lid and sides had eroded away.

"I don't know what I was thinkin'. Why did I even let ya go in there—" He shook his head. "Just look at ya."

I glanced down at myself. Red algae smeared the front of my gray sweatshirt, staining my knees and shins. Landan grunted and stormed away over the rocks toward the shore. I followed until our feet hit the beach pebbles.

"I'm sorry, Landan."

He didn't respond. I looked back at the rocks behind me. My heart sank.

What was I thinking? Why had I even come?

I sat down on a rock nearby, set the box on the ground, and brushed the rust from my hands. Landan stood close with his arms folded. The sun sank into the sea.

"Landan?" I waited, but he said nothing. "I do things like this. I don't know why. It's like at the airport. I just decided I was coming home. I didn't think. I didn't want to think. I wasn't even really sure why anyone but my dad would even care." I shivered as a twist of wind snaked down the back of my collar. "And, I just did it again."

He looked at me through the corner of his eyes. "It wasn't the cave that was the problem, Nora. It was the sudden spark in yer eye when ya saw that box. Ya could've fallen."

"I thought we'd found something important." I peered over at it. Now I had no desire to even open it. Aunt Nieve had died here. I'd hoped to find a reason for the curse, or maybe discover a missing piece to my family's history. Not sure I found anything. Not even sure why I dragged Landan along.

He would've believed me if something was strange or out of the ordinary.

"Can you tell me about the curse? You seemed to know something last time we talked."

His shoulders slumped, and his hands fell to his sides.

I stared at the pebbles, wishing I could bury my stupidity beneath them, then swallowed a hard lump rising in my throat. "Will the sluagh try to take my life too?"

Landan came over and sat beside me. He stared ahead, as though waiting for the waves to tell him to begin. "Listen. Demons and spirits are allowed ta have power over places." He swept his hand across the landscape. "This land has had its mix of spirits for hundreds of years. Faeries—haunts—gods. It doesn't affect all who live here, but it does those that make themselves vulnerable ta it. Are ya vulnerable, Nora?"

"I don't know what that means."

"Your great-gran opened the door ta them, but yer gran and Aunt Nieve kept that door wide open. Since yer gran's death, others have felt the surge of Balor's eye. His target had been focused, but then there was a void. Now . . . yer back. But"—he turned toward me—"that door *can* be shut, Nora."

"Balor is real?" My brows lifted and my hands squeezed my thighs.

"That's the name the Irish have given him."

"How did he get my mom?" I rocked back and forth, burying my head into my hands.

He tsked with a bitter twist in his mouth and stared back at the sea. "Still had the poison in her."

Poison?

"What did my great-grandmother do? How can I shut the door?"

He leaned over. "Do ya believe in witches?"

"Witches?" I asked.

"Yer great-grandmother had a friend. She dabbled in druidic craft. Dark magic. Thought she could help yer great-gran."

"Help her with what? Why?"

"She wanted ta get rid of yer great-gran's husband. He was a drunkard, and he hurt her."

I narrowed my eyes. "How can you possibly know that?"

"Dark magic never helps, Nora. It only hurts. Yer great-gran didn't understand."

"And you do? How?" I pressed my lips together, waiting for his reply. He said nothing. I shook my head. "Witches? Dark magic?" This started to rub me like sandpaper against soft wood. I could believe that something had happened with my family. But this? I stood to my feet. "What do you know, Landan? How do I know you aren't just making this all up?"

His whole face tightened, appearing frustrated as he rubbed his forehead. "What would I possibly gain from making up a story like this?"

"Then who told you?" I clenched my fists at my side. "How do you know so much about my family?"

He rose, lifting his hand as if trying to calm my storm. "Nora, I need ya ta trust me. There's a way ta stop all of this."

"Really? A way to stop my mom from dying?" Tears choked me. "To stop my dad from being a selfish, controlling jerk!"

Landan reached for me. I stepped away. He pulled his hand back. "I can't stop what has already been done."

"Then what can you do, Landan? You pop out of nowhere and tell me that there are witches . . . and . . . and . . . *demons*!"

"What do ya call what ya saw yesterday?"

I threw up my hands. "I don't know what I saw. Maybe I just lost my mind. Maybe I was seeing things."

"What about yer gran and Nieve? Were they just seeing t'ings?"

"My gran was a superstitious old woman. She blamed spirits for all the bad that happened. I'm not like her. Declan was right. The sluagh aren't real. None of it. It's all just been a cat in the window and a stupid girl grieving the death of her mom."

Landan stepped toward me again with an outstretched hand. "Please, Nora. Just—"

Declan.

I whipped my head toward the horizon. Dark blue hues filled the sky. My heart sank into my toes. We were supposed to go to dinner. Instead, I was dirty, damp, and with Landan. Nothing but a rusted metal box to show for it.

"Oh, my God!" I yelled. "It's so late. Declan probably saw I was gone and left." I grabbed the box, then dashed for The Flaherty House.

Maybe he'll be there.

15

Let's Be Honest

My lungs were on fire by the time I reached the trail that led to the house. Darkness blanketed everything—the sun asleep beneath the sealine. My chest heaved as I looked up at the ledge, but the landing was steeped in shadows.

I missed my date with Declan!

A gasping sob pushed out of my throat.

I can explain. He'll understand. We can just go out another day.

These thoughts fell like empty promises. In my *freak out* about the journal, I'd allowed myself to forget about Declan. Forget what really mattered. I thought about my dad, and how I'd left him in the lurch. He'd lost his wife too.

I shook my head, refusing to believe he deserved my grace or understanding.

With Declan on the other hand, it was me that might not deserve a second chance. My lungs burned in my chest, but it was my heart that turned inside out.

I'm a mess.

My curls were frayed every which way. I always had a hair-tie handy, so I set the box down and tried to smooth my hair up into a top knot. I pinched my cheeks to brighten them, but hopelessness hung like heavy weights from my chest. If I didn't have Declan anymore, how would I hold myself together?

Declan's been there for me. He'll understand—won't he?

I picked up the rusted box and started up the rocks toward the trail. The box weighed heavy like a scarlet letter. Maybe that was a bit extreme to think, but I'd forgotten Declan. No excuse could remove that mark. I hadn't even been a good friend.

My feet trudged up the trail. Maybe he'll be at the top with forgiving eyes, ready to hug me just like he had the day before. But when I emerged onto the landing, a different Declan awaited me. He sat slouched on the front step, his arms on his knees, with my jacket and journals beside him. Hurt lingered in his green eyes—disappointment etched his face.

"Declan." I ran over. "I'm so sorry. I didn't mean to forget dinner. I can explain."

He pursed his lips and held up his hands. "Ya know what, Nora—"

I held my breath.

"I know you've been going t'rough a lot, but"—he set his jaw—"you were wit' him, weren't ya?"

I nodded. "I was with Landan. But it's not what you—"

"Della said ya went off wit' him. I finally get it." He stood, pointing to the journals next to him. "Here's yer t'ings. Glad yer okay." He stormed toward his car.

I dropped the box. It hit the gravel with a sharp, splintering crash. I didn't care. I didn't even look at it as I chased after him. "No. No, Declan. Please don't leave."

"Nora, I am not goin' ta play these games wit' ya. The minute I'm gone, *he's always* there."

My face flushed cold.

I can't believe he would think that.

"It isn't like that with Landan. He's just a friend. Declan, you know him. You know what he's like."

"What are ya talkin' about?" Declan's tone was rough and raw, like gravel scraping over stone.

"What happened to the two of you, anyway? We used to all

play on the shore as kids. Now the two of you don't even speak? The mention of his name makes you *so* angry. I've seen it. Are you fighting?"

He peered at me over the top of his car, eyebrows raised like I was crazy. "Fightin'? Nora—what're ya sayin'? How can I be fightin' wit' someone I've never met? Don't even know what the git looks like."

"What? Of course you've seen him. When we were kids, he—"

"There was *never* anyone wit' us. It was just us. The two of us." He glared at me like I made it all up.

"But—"

"No one named Landan lives in this village!" Declan snapped.

I gasped. Tears welled in my eyes.

He dropped his head and cocked his jaw, seeming shocked at his own outburst. "I've checked."

"But I remember him. He was there. I saw him." I dredged through my memories for the moments he was with us—moments when Declan would have been with him. I came up empty. Landan hovered in the background like a ghost. My heart skipped faster.

He was there. This is nonsense.

Declan's car door creaked open. I snapped to attention and jetted around the front of his car. "Landan. You don't remember Landan?"

"There. Is. No. Landan." Declan's face reddened as clear anger and hurt ebbed in his eyes. He ran his hand over his face. "At least none I've ever met."

I gulped. Confusion and fear grappled for my attention.

He's getting into his car.

I scrambled over to hold the car door open.

"Please, just give me a moment to explain. There is nothing to be jealous of."

Declan's eyes flared. "Jealous!"

I stepped back. Tears dripped from my eyes.

What do I need to say to make him stay?

Declan's mouth tightened. "I am *not* jealous, Nora. I am just not going ta—"

"Not going to what? Not going to fight for me?" Sobs bent me over, and I struggled to breath.

No. I can't lose it. Get him to stay.

I straightened, thrusting my hands over my mouth to hold my erupting emotions inside. "You're right." I lowered my hands with an exhale. "I don't know what I'm doing. I learned that tonight. I just do things without thinking." I lifted my chin as another surge of emotion threatened to burst free. I couldn't meet the fiery accusation burning in Declan's eyes.

My feet fumbled back, retreating without my permission. "I'm not going to do that anymore. Lesson learned." The unyielding wall Declan raised put my chest in a stranglehold. The house was my only safe place now. I turned my back and stumbled toward it.

I waited for the car door to slam shut and the engine to roar to life. My eyes lifted to the upstairs window. It was open again. The curtains plumed out like arms ready to pull me inside.

This is where I belong. I'm cursed like the rest of the women in my family.

Images of when Declan and I were kids tugged at my shattering heart. Declan's arm around me when my gran died. His laughter as we splashed in the waves. It was always worth the punishment I would receive for getting my uniform wet.

Wait. Try again. Be honest before he drives away.

I spun back around. Declan's eyes had softened, but his lips were still a tense line. "You're right, you know," I hollered. "You aren't the jealous one. When we were kids, I used to hate it when you'd build those dumb rock towers. You were always so proud of them, but they would make me so mad."

Declan's eyes narrowed, a flicker of confusion crossing his face.

"You'd spend hours looking at them, building them taller and taller. I just wanted you to look at me." Another sob clogged my throat. "I knocked them all down because I was *jealous*. You'd be so angry, but I didn't care, because I had your attention again."

I wiped my sweatshirt sleeves across my cheeks. The honesty tempered my storm, and I could breathe again.

"I didn't know why I jumped on that plane to come here. I thought it was because I missed my mom—my gran—or this house. I thought it might have been because I wanted to find something I used to have. But then I had to ask myself: Why do I want to stay when all those things are gone? Why do I want to stay even though I'm haunted by some evil spirit?" I avoided Declan's response to my last question and stared up at the twinkling stars.

"I realized it today. Or maybe I have a little every day since I've been back. But the truth is, I don't want to leave because *you're* here. I don't want to leave because I think what I was searching for was your doorstep." A long, hard breath pushed me forward, and I wrapped my arms around my stomach. No one had ever been as safe or warm as Declan. "You're my home, Declan. Not Landan. He's just someone I used to know. I–l—"

My swallow stole my voice when I spoke again; I hardly made a sound. "I love you." I couldn't say it again. I was about to burst.

I sniffed, the cool air turning my tear-streaked cheeks to ice, but I'd said it. I'd heard the words fall from my lips, and I hoped Delan heard them too.

I still couldn't face him and kept my gaze elsewhere. The thought of his rejection staring back at me was unbearable. My heart was as fragile as glass; one unforgiving look and it would shatter. I turned away and retreated to the house.

I opened the door but did not go inside right away, hoping Delcan might be right behind me. He never came. Only a frigid breeze on the back of my shoulders.

Maybe he'll forgive me in a few days.

I crossed the threshold and closed the door behind me. Declan's car ignited outside. My heart cracked wider. Sobs bubbled up, craving to be set free. I held them in as tight as I could and wandered aimlessly toward the kitchen, desperate to turn my feelings off.

What do I do?

The thick weight of my despair pulled me into a chair at the dining room table. I buried my face in my hands.

My phone was within reach. I peered between my fingers at the screen. Ten text messages and more missed calls. I sighed, reaching for it and unlocking the screen. There were a few texts from friends at college checking in on me, but most were from my dad.

James Morrigan (Dad):

"Thanks for the thumbs up. At least I know you're okay."

"I know we've had some hard times, but I do care about you. We need to fix this."

"I worry that you went back to school too quickly. I haven't been back to work. Nothing is normal anymore."

"Please call me. I just want to talk."

I rubbed my eyes. I couldn't keep reading Dad's messages. The guilt that clung to me was already more than I could handle. I folded my arms on the table and buried my head in them. Muffled sobs wracked my body.

I wish I could rewind time and stop myself from running off with Landan.

My tears flooded free, drowning me beneath waves of pain and regret. Just like in the cave all those years ago, Declan's hand floated away from me—the black torrent dragging me out to sea. The bracelet he'd given me—gone. I had nothing left.

The door clicked, startling me.

I lifted my head.

Declan walked inside.

My heart pounded through my chest as I wiped away tears.

He stood in the doorway and didn't come closer. His eyes were red, lashes wet, and his arms were folded across his chest.

I stayed frozen in my seat. I didn't want to do anything that might make him leave.

"I, eh"—he cleared his throat—"was really angry." He pursed his lips. "I t'ink, somehow, ya runnin' off wit' that bloke today made me feel t'ings I haven't since, em—since the day yer da ripped ya away." His chin trembled.

I couldn't help it. The look in his eye pulled me to my feet.

"I *was* jealous." A muscle rippled in his jaw. "I wanted to rip his . . . Landan's arms off. But . . . that's daft, right?" Declan kicked the floor with his shoes. "I read that journal entry yer gran wrote. The one ya left sittin' on the table at Della's. I can see why that upset ya." He paused, staring at the floor. "Where did ya go?" His eyes begged for me to say something that would quell his storm.

"I, um . . . I went to the cave."

"What?" Declan's voice rose in pitch. "You went back to that dangerous place?"

"My—my Aunt Nieve drowned there."

Declan nodded. "I know. You almost did too. Why would you go back?"

"I wanted to see the place where she died. It was stupid. I know." I spread out my arms, displaying my muddied clothes. "Really slippery. I almost fell."

His eyes widened and his jaw slackened. "You went in?"

"Landan came with me."

Declan pinched the bridge of his nose and shut his eyes.

"I–I didn't seek him out. I would've gone by myself. He's always just there. And—" I looked away. "He believes me," I whispered.

Declan's whole face tightened. "About the sluagh?"

I nodded, my face heating as I admitted it. "I went a little crazy after reading about my aunt. It—it scared me."

He stood in silence, staring at the floor as the seconds dragged on. Doubt gnawed at me—had I said enough? Or maybe too much?

Finally, he nodded and lifted his gaze. "I am—so sorry, Nora." He moved toward me. "I didn't believe ya. I've left ya alone in this, and then I wonder why it's Landan that is there instead of me."

I shook my head. "No—no. You've been the only one here for me. That is not how it is."

"It is," he said, moving even closer until he stood in front of me. "Somet'ing *is* happenin', Nora. I don't want ta believe it's the sluagh, but I don't t'ink yer mad either. Nor do I t'ink yer makin' stuff up—especially not after readin' what yer gran wrote. I've left ya ta figure it out alone. I would've never done that when we were kids."

A sob caught in my chest. "But we aren't kids anymore."

"No." His hand cradled my chin while the other sifted hair over my ear. "We aren't kids anymore."

My gaze centered on his. His eyes, no longer angry, now held the yearning I longed for. "I'm so sorry," he whispered, leaning closer. His hand slipped from my chin to caress my cheek.

My heart fluttered in my chest. "You have nothing to be sorry for."

His breath quickened as the tip of his nose brushed mine, drawing me into his warmth. The nerves on my lips and cheeks burned. Words tangled in my throat—I wanted to say something, anything, to tell him I never wanted to leave him again. But he said it first.

"I've been in love wi't ya my whole life, Nora Morrigan." His brows lifted with his words. His green eyes glistened as a single tear slipped down his cheek. "I don't want ta push ya away. Or let"—his eyes squeezed shut—"Landan have ya."

I lifted my chin. My lips almost touched his. Every part of me longed to be that much closer. His hands slid past my jaw—his fingers threading through my hair—then he pressed his lips against mine. I rose onto my toes, pulling him closer with my hands wrapped behind his neck. The heat of his lips sent tingles racing across my skin. His breath, his need apparent, as he pulled me closer, stirred something buried deep inside me—something that had always been there.

I love him too.

He pulled his lips away, and I instinctively leaned in to follow. But then his smile caught my gaze, and its warmth lit me on the inside. "I've been wanting you to do that since yesterday."

His sigh feathered my cheek. "Well, I've been wantin' ta kiss ya for longer than I'd like ta admit."

The complete contentment in his eyes stole away all I thought I'd lost from my stupid mistake. "Sorry I ruined dinner."

He chuckled, pressing his forehead to mine. His fingers slid down my shoulders to the middle of my back. I cupped his firm chin and closed my eyes, breathing him in. Peppermint. It lingered there on his breath.

"Thanks for not leaving." I opened my eyes, searching his. "I'm such an idiot sometimes."

"Yer not an idiot. Impulsive, though—well, I guess that one's not new." He lifted his head. Obvious apprehension shadowed his eyes as he stared at the door.

"What's wrong?"

He didn't say anything.

I cupped his face in my hands, guiding his gaze away from the door and back to me. "I swear, Dec, Landan is nothing—barely even a friend."

He kissed the top of my head. "That's not what's troublin' me anymore."

"What is it, then?"

"It's the fact that no one has seen him but yerself."

"Della saw him."

He nodded. "Della did. But that is the first time she's ever set eyes on him."

16

Buttons

No one besides me and Della has ever seen Landan?

My face fell. "That doesn't make any sense?"

"No, it doesn't," Declan said, glaring at the window.

"That can't be right. Landan's been here for as long as I can remember."

Declan tore his gaze from the window, shaking his head. "No. He hasn't. That's what I'm tryin' ta tell ya, Nora. I would've seen him, or at least heard of him. Me da has his nose into everyone's business being the postmaster, and even he was baffled."

"You told your dad about him?"

The whole village is going to think I'm crazy.

"Had to ask him. Been weird ta me ever since ya first mentioned him."

"Well, he's real. I was just with him."

"Yah." Declan's glare deepened. "Somethin' about yer gran's journal has me t'inkin'." He walked to the window and peered in both directions. "She talked about that boy. The one with a nice face but the devil in his eyes."

"Declan. Landan's not—"

"A shape-shifter? That's what yer gran called that boy." He turned to face me, snapping his fingers as though trying to remember the name Gran had used. "A daoine maithe."

My eyes widened. "A faery? Now who's the crazy one? Landan doesn't have evil in his eyes. And he is certainly not a gancanagh, deceiving me with his beauty. If anything, I'm always just making him angry. There isn't any alluring spell."

"What do ya mean?" He turned around and grabbed each of my arms. His eyes searched mine.

"He's always scolding me for not being more careful. He didn't want me to go into the cave today. I went anyway, and then he yelled at me for risking my safety to get that box."

The box! I left it outside!

I joined Declan at the window. The rusty box lay on the ground just shy of the trail. The bottom had shattered, rust-colored debris scattered beneath it.

I stepped away from the window. "Besides, there is no gancanagh or sluagh. I think I've just let my imagination run away—"

A black shadow leapt into the window frame. I screamed, thrusting myself into Declan's arms. Buttons sat on the windowsill licking his lips.

"STUPID CAT!" I screamed. I pointed at him through the windowpane. "I swore I'd toss you over that cliff if you scared me again. All this talk about shape-shifters, and that's when *you* decide to jump up. Gawd!"

Declan chuckled. "He probably saw ya at the window and hoped you'd bring him some supper."

I shook my head. "No supper for you," I growled at Buttons.

"What's in the box, anyway?" Declan asked.

"I don't know. I saw it in the cave—hoped it might be a clue or something. I didn't have time to open it. I was worried about getting back to you." I tilted my head to meet Declan's eyes. He grinned, then leaned down and gave me another soft kiss. When he pulled back, I bit my bottom lip. "Still really sorry about all that."

"I know. But the next time I ask ya out—how 'bout ya don't run off?"

"The next time?" I batted my eyes at him.

"Course." He dipped in for another kiss. I loved the feel of his lips and hated it when he pulled away again. Now I was leaning into Della's idea of snogging. He flicked his chin toward the window. "Should we go collect that box, then?"

"Yeah, well"—I stepped back, motioning down at my muddied clothes—"I think I should freshen up first."

"Right." He pulled his lips to one side, looking me up and down. "Ya're a right mess. I'll get the box. You get changed."

I slipped into a clean pink T-shirt, followed by a warm cardigan and my cozy black stretch pants. I let out a breath.

Maybe I'll make us some sandwiches with the leftover ham.

I still hadn't eaten, and I was sure Declan hadn't either. A small swirl of unease lingered in my stomach over what had happened, but perhaps some food and the warmth of a fire would help.

I grabbed my dirty clothes and headed to the washer in the kitchen. Strange place for a washer and dryer, but all the Irish had them in their kitchens. The big refrigerators and laundry rooms were an American thing I'd grown accustomed to.

I traipsed past the stairwell. The door was closed, but a chilly draft wafted over my bare feet from underneath the crack.

Oh! I need to shut that window!

The knot that usually tightened in my stomach wasn't there, as if the fear of the upstairs had become nothing more than a long-forgotten dream.

I'll close it later.

I wandered into the dining room. The rusted box sat on the table with other orangish-red bits and pieces. I couldn't wait to take a closer look. But where was Declan? I glanced around and shrugged. Maybe he was still outside gathering anything else that fell out of the box.

I loaded the washer, filled the soap, and started the laundry. I leaned against the counter, waiting for Declan, the gentle whir of the washer in my ears. Five minutes or more passed.

Where is he?

I left the kitchen and checked the front door.

"Declan?"

Nothing.

"Hm?"

Strange.

I went over to the window. Declan stood outside on the front steps, holding the cat's bowl. Kibble lay scattered across the ground. Something about the way he stood, frozen, sent a trickle of fear through my blood.

I rushed to the door and opened it. I touched his arm. "Dec? Is everything okay?" I scanned the darkness, then looked up at him. "Where's Buttons?"

His eyes flickered, wide with fright—like he'd seen Balor himself.

"Declan?" I stepped in front of him, grabbing both of his arms and shaking him. "What happened? Are you all right?"

His head turned toward the upstairs windows. "We need ta shut those windows."

His dilated pupils dipped to meet mine. Coldness crept through my whole body. Prickles of terror quickened my breathing. "N-No," I stuttered. "Everything"—I shook my head—"everything is fine."

"Get in the house," Declan said, grabbing my shoulders.

"What?"

"GET IN THE HOUSE—NOW, NORA!" Declan shoved me inside, then turned and locked the door behind him. He rushed over to the large front window and pulled the curtains shut. "Do ya have the keys?"

"What's happening?"

"The keys, Nora. To the upstairs." He held out his hand, eyes wide and pleading. My mind froze, unable to form a single thought. The fear etched into Declan's face sent me into a dark spiral. He'd always been so brave. I couldn't process the sudden emergency. My tongue was tied.

"NORA!"

I pulled the words out one at a time. "It's . . . it's . . . not . . . locked."

"Find the keys." Declan dashed away. His footfalls pounded up the creaking stairs.

My feet carried me to the kitchen counter, where the keys lay waiting. I fumbled to grab them, my fingers scraping against the cold metal. I secured them in my grip right as Declan emerged from the hallway once more.

I lifted the keys; they rattled in my shaky hand. "Keys."

He grabbed them and disappeared into the hallway. I folded my hands to hold them still. Tears welled in my eyes as Declan reappeared, backing out of the hallway. He shut that door too, then turned the lock.

I couldn't stand it a second more. "Declan," I cried, tears swimming in my vision. "What's happening? You're frightening me."

He spun around. His eyes darted right and left, his mouth gaping as he caught his breath. "It's"—he swallowed, reaching for me—"going ta be okay." He pulled me close to his chest and kissed the top of my head.

No. This isn't right.

Declan held onto me like predators were about to snatch me from his arms. I squeezed his jumper, afraid to speak.

"It's okay," he puffed, still gasping for breath. "I t'ink it's okay now." He stepped back, cupping my cheeks. He wiped a tear away with his thumb. "Don't cry, Nora. I'm goin' ta keep ya safe."

I stepped back. "What are you talking about? What happened?"

"I'm sorry I didn't believe ya, okay? But I'm not goin' ta lose ya. Tomorrow we're goin' ta get ya on a plane back home."

"What?" My knees crumbled beneath me, but Declan caught me by my elbows. "No—I won't go," I bellowed.

"We don't have a choice."

Fight rose up in me, and I pushed him back. "Declan. Why are you acting like this? You need to talk to me right now. I'm not having this." Images of my dad taking me by the arm and shoving me in the car pounded my brain. My teeth clenched. "I'm not letting anyone take me away again! I would rather die!" Flames must have blazed in my eyes because Declan stood back and held up his hands. "You of all people should know that. If you don't tell me what is going on, I'm going straight out that door *right now*."

Declan inhaled a deep breath, stood taller, and rubbed his hands over his face. He bit into his bottom lip, his eyes moistening. "It—it was the cat. It was Buttons."

The lights flickered, and then they went out.

17

Someone's at the Door

The tumble of the washing machine came to a halt. Everything fell silent. The wind whirred outside. Declan's hands found me in the dark and pulled me close.

Bam, bam, bam!

Someone pounded at the door. My body tensed. Declan's grip tightened. Our huffing breath escaped into the stillness. The rising wind outside swelled into an unrelenting, ghostly moan.

Bam, bam!

I yelped, burying my face into Declan's chest. My mind raced—who was it?

"Nora! Ya need ta let me in!" a voice called.

"It's Landan," I whispered to Declan.

He held a finger to his lips. "Don't let him in."

Bam, bam, bam.

"Nora!" Landan called again. "Let me in. It'll be okay. Ya need ta trust me."

I fondled the rosary around my wrist. Declan kept me locked in his embrace, as if he had no intention of letting me near the door.

But Landan's only ever helped me.

"Declan, it's just Landan."

Declan's face turned ashen. "No, it's not," he said, clutching me even tighter.

Bam, bam, bam.

I stifled another scream into Declan's shoulder. "Who is it then?"

"I don't know." The quaver in Declan's voice churned my insides. "It was Buttons, and then—"

"Nora! Please . . . listen ta me," Landan's familiar voice pleaded, before the storm's howl swallowed it away.

The assailing wind blew in from the fireplace, wailing, *"N-O-R-A!"* The banshee-like cry shook me to my core.

Declan's breath clipped as though he'd heard it too.

I pressed my palms over my ears. Glass shattered upstairs, then a thump tumbled across the ceiling. It didn't sound like footsteps—images of a corpse rolling over the floor made me clench my teeth.

Bang, bang, bang hounded us from the front door.

I need to let Landan in.

I yanked toward the door.

"No, Nora." Delcan held me tight.

Thumps rolled across the upstairs floorboards.

He's found me. Balor found me. It's all real.

I wished I could disappear—retreat to the safety of my life at university, aimlessly drifting from class to class. Where had that life gone? My mother's death had stolen it all away.

What if I'd just gone back to school instead of coming here? Would any of this be happening then? I don't want to die.

The stairs creaked. Footfalls thudded down the stairwell until they smashed into the locked door. I cringed, clinging tighter to Declan with each reverberating slam.

"N-O-R-A!" The wind's echo boomed through the house.

CRASH!

Something hit the hallway door. I screamed. Declan let go, leaving me without his arms for security. Darkness surrounded me like a chilling void as I searched for a corner to hide. The hall doorknob jostled. Declan's shadowed figure darted toward the hallway door.

"Nora! Let me in!" Landan's voice barely rose over the pummeling wind.

I can't keep ignoring him!

His voice tore through my mind, tugging at me like an invisible magnet.

Delcan gripped the doorknob, holding it fast. He groaned, wrestling against whatever lurked on the other side. The door banged against his hold. My hands clenched my ears. The curse had come for me. The sluagh—or Balor—was inside the house about to break down the door.

A tight, weakening groan eked from Declan that ripped through the depths of my soul. Fear, not for myself but for Declan, snapped me into action. I sprang toward the front door.

"No, Nora!" Declan screamed, his body pressed against the hallway door.

I turned the lock and reached for the knob.

The rising crescendo of all three voices—Declan, Landan, the sluagh—calling my name drove me into a frenzy. I flung open the door. A tympanic burst vibrated the air. A flood of wind careened into the house, knocking me back. My head crashed into the wall behind me. White dots blurred my vision, and I slumped to the floor. The blazing gale rushed over me, ripping through the room with ruthless force. Sheer panic seized me, its icy claws sinking deep, like shards of glass slicing through my veins.

What have I done?

Was this it? Was I about to breathe my last? What about Declan?

He isn't cursed. Maybe he'll be okay.

I didn't know how to pray, but my fingers turned the beads

of the rosary—my heart beseeching the God of my Aunt Nieve to save me. To save us.

All at once, the wind turned from a rage to a whisper. My furling hair came to rest around my face. My panting breath resonated in my ears. The lights flickered back on.

"Declan!" I screamed, tears streaming from my eyes. The wind had overturned the sofa and pushed it across the room. My gran's lamp and side table lay lopsided on the floor. One peacock remained sideways on the wall; the other one had fallen somewhere out of sight.

My eyes landed on the hallway door. A splintering crack ran down the middle. The back of my head throbbed. I reached behind to touch it—a warm wetness met my fingertips.

"Declan," I called again, too shaken to move. I stared out the front door into the inky blackness. No Landan. No Buttons. No sluagh. No more sign of a raging wind—just a cold breeze and the quiet night's sky.

"Ugh . . . " Declan moaned from across the room. "Ah." His body shifted against the floor.

"Declan—Declan! Are you okay?"

His hand reached over the sofa's backrest, and he pulled himself up. His right arm was curled against his chest. Declan's shoulders heaved with his breath as he scanned the room. When his eyes met mine, a relieved exhale doubled him over. He caught himself with his left hand on the back of the sofa.

My heart squeezed. This was my fault. Declan was hurt, and I was responsible. My great- grandmother's curse didn't belong to him. He shouldn't have to protect me—or himself—from it. My face fell into my hands as tears rushed from my eyes.

"Nora," he said, breathless. His heavy steps shuffled toward me, scraping the floor like a staggering undead. He collapsed beside me and reached for my cheek. His lips met mine in a fleeting kiss, mingling my relief with a heavy anvil of remorse.

A deep sob burst from my lips. "I'm sorry, Declan. I needed to let him in."

His sad eyes held mine as his brows lifted. "Yer sorry?" His voice was labored as he struggled to catch his breath. He pulled me close with his good arm, cradling the back of my head. "Whatever ya did—it stopped everyt'in'."

"Do you think it's over?"

"I don't know." He exhaled, looking around the room. "All I know is I wasn't going ta be able ta hold that door much longer."

I whimpered. "Is your arm okay?"

"It's fine. It's—"

He stopped short, sitting up as his gaze shifted to the hand that cradled my head. My blood painted his palm. "Damn, Nora. Yer bleedin'. Can we not keep ya from bleedin' for even a day?"

I sniffled. "I'm fine."

"Sure yer not fine." He tilted my head back and scanned my eyes, as though checking if my pupils were dilated.

"Well, neither are you. None of this is fine, Declan. What the hell has my great-gran unleashed upon me?"

He wiped his hand on his dark gray jumper, the red vanishing into the black. "That's why we need ta get ya out of here. Ya can't stay, Nora."

My chin trembled. "But my mom left and she died anyway."

I can't outrun this.

"She might've just gotten sick," he said, his eyes pleading for me to give him the simple answer.

"No." I shook my head. "The poison just took its time. Same as Gran. That's what Landan said, anyway."

Declan froze at the mention of Landan's name. His gaze whipped toward the open door.

"But that isn't what happened to Aunt Nieve. I hate to think what might have actually happened to her." I scrunched my face, the sluagh chasing me to the edge of the cliff replaying in my mind. There wasn't any point questioning whether the sluagh were real now. "I wonder how my great-gran died. There was nothing in the journals about it—or anything that could've prepared me for *this*. Why is it so strong? What have I done to make this happen?"

Declan's face flushed with a storm of emotions, as though wrestling with the weight of my words.

"You can just leave me here. Let Balor take me. Then at least you'll be okay."

He clenched his jaw. "Shut yer mouth. I won't hear ya say that."

"But what else can I do? I saw them." I wrapped my arms around my middle.

"Saw who?"

"The sluagh. Yesterday. Declan, I didn't just accidentally run off the edge of the cliff. They chased me. They were like massive black crows, clamoring after me."

Declan slumped his head into his hands. "I would've never believed ya."

"I didn't believe me either. Landan said—"

"Nora," Declan cut me off, his gaze serious. "Landan is not—"

"He's not what?" I interjected. "Landan said he could help. That I needed to trust him. That the door of this curse could be closed."

Declan's shoulders drooped. "How?"

I spilled everything that Landan had told me about the curse and the witch's dark magic. Declan seemed to take it all in stride. His jaw clenched tight as he listened, staring into the cold night.

When I finished, he got up and shut the front door. He turned, held out his hand, and helped me from the floor.

"How ya feel? Dizzy?"

I shook my head. "I'm fine," I said, even though the dizziness lingered and my head throbbed. I didn't want him to worry.

"Let's get ya cleaned up." He peered over his shoulder at the cracked hall door, rubbing his upper arm and shoulder with a hiss. "Do you think it will come back?"

I shrugged. I didn't know.

"Nora?" He slipped his hands into his pockets, casting a sidelong glance in my direction.

"Yeah?"

"What does Landan look like?"

I blinked, arranging his features in my mind. "He . . . um . . . he has dark, raven-black hair. Wears a peacoat."

He squinted. "Longer hair?"

I nodded.

Declan pressed his lips together. "I think I saw him—before all this happened. Buttons was there"—he pointed to the door—"and then all at once—"

He stopped, his mouth twisting as though he couldn't believe his own words. "The cat was gone and then *he* stood in front of me."

"He?" I pulled Declan's arm for him to look at me. "You mean, Landan? You saw him?"

His eyes connected with mine, and he nodded. "He's the one that told me ta shut the windows, and that *it* was comin' for ya."

"For me?" My fingers dug into my arms. "Who was coming? Balor?"

Declan dropped his gaze to the floor. "He didn't say." His fists clenched and unclenched at his sides. "It was like a trick of the eye. There were black wings, and then . . . "

Dread widened my eyes.

"Nothin'." He lifted his eyes back to mine. "Landan— he *shifted*. Do ya understand what I'm tellin' ya? If I hadn't seen it wit' my own eyes, I would t'ink it was all mad. He's a gancanagh." He lifted the curtain with his finger, peered out one more time, then let it drop. "But I t'ink yer right. I t'ink he wants ta help. That's unless he's foolin' us both, and all this was just a trick. A trap."

My mind flashed to the cave, when Landan had said, *"like a rabbit in a trap."*

"If he's a gancanagh," Declan continued, "it may be the very one that yer gran separated from yer Aunt Nieve. Maybe her words are a warning to us."

"Or—maybe she was wrong. Nieve died without him by her side."

We need to find Landan—and fast.

18

Great-Gran's Daughters

I sat in front of the burning fireplace with a fleece blanket wrapped around my shoulders. One arm hugged my legs to my chest, while the other pressed a package of frozen peas against the back of my head.

Why don't I feel better?

Declan had seen it all now—I wasn't alone anymore, and I wasn't crazy. But somehow it seemed worse, like I was this plagued thing that shouldn't be touched. That I was poison, even.

Declan had pushed the sofa against the hallway door. I didn't blame him. The simple barricade helped ease our troubled minds.

Though I doubt it'd be enough to hold Balor back if he comes again.

The house was in disarray, similar to how my insides felt—wrecked. Declan sat with his back against the wall, massaging his arm, his face tense. I couldn't shake the images of my death out of my head: blazing over the edge of the cliff, almost slipping into the hungry mouth of the cave. If Landan hadn't been there—

I squeezed my eyes shut, dipping my chin to my chest. "I don't want to die."

Declan lifted his head up from the wall. "Yer not goin' ta die."

I couldn't look at him. I loved him—but what had I done by letting him into my life now? "You can't know that."

"I've got a plan."

What could he possibly do?

I kept my thoughts to myself. I needed Declan to have hope.

"We won't be stayin' here another day. That's the first t'ing."

I peered over at him. Thoughts swirled behind his irises.

"It seems the curse is on *this* house too—not just you. No point stayin' here. It's like leavin' ya wide open for it all ta happen again." He paused like there was a bad taste in his mouth.

"Should we leave right now?" I asked.

A faint, windy moan echoed outside. Declan twisted his lips. "Yes. He might come back."

Who is he? Balor? The sluagh?

From what Gran told me, Balor sent the harbingers of death. Once the sluagh called, Balor would claim the soul. I still wasn't sure what the curse had created, only that *he . . . it . . .* wanted to kill me because of the curse.

"And then, we need ta find Landan," Declan finally said. "If he says there's a way ta stop all this, then we need ta find out what it is."

I bit the inside of my cheek. "He's a demon."

"He's a demon wit' answers."

My jaw fell open.

I can't believe he's defending Landan.

I couldn't help but agree, though. I should've been more afraid of Landan, but like Declan—I wasn't. The Landan of my nightmares could've been Balor himself. The devil. An angel in the guise of light. But he *did* seem to be the only one who knew anything.

"Also," Declan said, pushing himself onto his feet. He made his way to the kitchen, lifted my dad's black journal from the counter, and wiggled it back and forth. "I've been t'inkin' about this. We need ta read it. Might have somet'ing important."

I rolled my eyes.

"Nora—we can't leave any rock unturned. We have it. We should read it." He looked at the door, then offered his hand. "We should go."

I nodded, removing the package of thawed peas, and prodding the knot on the back of my head. There was a cut, but it was small—just a bleeder. I took his hand, and he pulled me to my feet.

"How's the head?"

"It's fine," I grumbled.

Declan chuckled. "Grand. Nothin' that a packet of mushy peas can't handle."

I glowered at him, and he laughed a bit more. But then, his face turned serious. "Really glad it wasn't worse."

I shrugged, not having anything more to give. Declan's smiles and charming demeanor just drove the nail deeper into my heart. Somehow, I would lose him, or he would lose me. I struggled to maintain any optimism that I would get through this, and I wanted him as far away from it as possible.

His eyes were on me, but I ignored him.

Once we're away from here, tell him to leave. Tell him to never come back.

I didn't possess the strength to tell him, though.

I don't want to be alone. But . . . How selfish can I be?

Maybe since he wasn't the one cursed, it would all pass him by, like a rock surrounded by the high tide. Come the relenting water, the rock would still stand.

Not sure that's a risk worth taking.

"Come on," he said, pulling me to his side. "Let's get out of here."

I peered behind me as we walked toward the door.

Does any of the stuff in this house even matter?

Declan removed his arm, jostling his car keys in his palm. He shot me a reassuring grin and reached for the doorknob.

It didn't turn. Declan's brows pinched, and his eyes narrowed toward the door. "Is it locked?" He twisted the lock. It moved freely. He jostled the knob again, but it held fast. "What in the—"

I stepped back. My jaw locked and my body tensed. I turned toward the kitchen.

Declan was already ahead of me. He scrambled toward the kitchen's back door.

I didn't follow. A new wave of fear mounted inside me. My nails dug into my arms as the door rattled without opening.

Declan backtracked away from the kitchen door. His face was blank as he combed his hand through his hair before covering his mouth.

My voice squeezed in my throat. "Is it stuck too?"

He didn't answer but shuffled to the window, lifted the curtain, then whipped it shut. He spun around to face me.

"W-What did you see?"

His eyes swiveled back and forth as though his mind didn't want to believe it. He shook his head, cast the journal to the floor, then tried the front door again. He shook the doorknob. Angst tightened his lips, exposing his clenched teeth as he rattled the knob.

"Ah," he hissed, pulling his arm into his chest, then kicked the door.

I swallowed hard. Any feeble word of comfort escaped me. I wanted to crawl in a corner and hide. My breath quickened with another onset of tears.

We're trapped.

"What's out there?" I asked.

Declan's breath heaved with obvious frustration. "Fog."

"Oh." I nodded, and a single tear dripped down my cheek. "It was a clear night."

His eyelids lowered. "It's not anymore. Ya can't go out there. Not even if I could figure out how ta get us out. It's not just fog."

It's cursed.

He stared up at the ceiling. "Not going up there either. Windows open." He rubbed his forehead as though still working out what to do.

My shoulders slumped.

I'm so tired from all of it.

I wandered toward the fireplace, wrapped the blanket around my shoulders, and nestled on the floor next to the warmth. I was ready to curl into myself—hide away from the blaring reality that threatened us both.

A grunt came from Declan. He'd taken his phone out and tried to make a call. He glared at the rectangular device as if deciding whether to throw it across the room. "No service," he said through clenched teeth. "It's like we're in some sort of void."

"At least there's no wind. M-Maybe that means we're okay," I said, allowing myself that small hope.

His pursed lips loosened, and he snatched my dad's journal from the floor. "We have something. We have this." With a stubborn look in his eye, he ambled into the living room and sat on the floor.

The flickering flames of the fireplace kept my mind distracted, and the peat moss crumbled.

He lifted the journal up after ten minutes or so. "I'm not going ta sit here and do nothin'."

"You read it," I said, tucking my hands over my ears as if that would magically block out my dad's words. I had no more resources to deal with my dad's journaled sentiments.

"Nora?"

I didn't look at him.

He sighed in obvious concession. He wasn't going to force me to drop my walls toward my dad. Not right now, anyway.

The rustle of thumbed pages pricked my curiosity. I peeked through the corner of my eye. Declan sat with the journal open in his lap, turning to the bookmarked pages. His eyes flicked to meet mine, then back at the page, as though pretending he hadn't noticed me staring.

I eyed the window and pulled the blanket tighter around my shoulders, then turned back to Declan.

His fingers filtered through the pages, his eyes scanning up and down until—"Ah," he muttered, narrowing in on whatever passage captured his attention. "Figured I should go back a little."

My curiosity surged as Declan's brows knitted together, his eyes scrolling back and forth. It gnawed at me to sit quietly and resist the urge to sneak over and read the journal for myself. But then—all the excuses my dad had made for himself during our drive to the airport replayed in my mind. How he'd refused to take responsibility for his actions. His control had decimated me—had decimated Mom. I didn't want to hear the tone of his voice echoed in his written words.

Declan's breath hitched, and his mouth gaped.

I lifted my head. "What?"

His eyes met mine, but then he turned back to the page and kept reading.

My curiosity percolated to the point I no longer cared that we were trapped. "Tell me."

He shushed me.

I groaned. What could my dad possibly have to say that would interest me?

My clients this . . . blah blah blah. The business needs this . . . blah blah blah. Ugh. Did he ever talk about anything else?

I fumed even thinking about my dad's usual rhetoric.

Declan leaned in closer. His eyes darted faster across the pages. He flipped one page after another. His face fell, and I scooted across the floor to peek at the journal.

"Wait." He held up his hand. "Trust me. Just a minute."

I smirked, then nodded and settled in front of him.

He stole a deep breath and smacked the journal shut. His head leaned back against the wall as he pinched his thumb and fingers over his eyes.

"You're killing me," I said.

He shoved the journal beneath his legs like he didn't want me to have it.

"You can't keep it from me."

He shook his head, pulling his lips into a wry grin.

"Declan." I leaned forward to grab the journal, but he shooed my hand away.

"I'm not going ta keep it from ya. It's just . . . " He rubbed his neck. His eyes flickered toward the window and then the door. "Let me process for a minute."

"Will it help us, or just make me angry?"

"It, uh . . . Maybe both."

"Declan? Tell me what that means."

"Maybe, ya just let me tell ya what I read first, and then you can have it."

"Okay," I said, giving in. "But why is that different?"

"I think it might hit ya different—me tellin ya, verses ya readin' it. If that makes sense." The skin on his throat reddened, and his eyes were wary.

"You mean, filter out the stuff that might upset me?"

"Em? Not filter per say. It's just so direct. Sort of"—he searched for the words—"without empathy."

"Yeah." I dropped my head. "I know exactly what you mean now." That snatched the curiosity right out of me. My dad had a way of seeming so disconnected from what everyone else went through. So cerebral and impartial. I took a deep breath, preparing myself. "So, let's have it, then."

Declan placed his folded arms on his knees, his nearness cuing me to scoot closer. The fire needed more peat and was cooling. The coldness of the window stole my comfort and reminded me we were not entirely alone. "Yer da's entries are short. Not a whole lot of detail."

"Okay?"

"Starts off grumblin' about yer gran. Says she's gotten worse since her husband died, talkin' about some curse." He motioned toward the window. "He said that yer gran was fillin' yer ma wit' ideas—tellin' her about yer great-gran and such. Anyway"—Declan rolled his shoulders and neck—"he t'ought it was all nonsense. But yer ma seemed ta believe it. That really upset him."

"Makes sense. Sounds like him."

"Yer gran was startin' ta say t'ings like her time was short and that Una needed to pay attention ta"—he hesitated—"what would start ta happen ta ya."

"To me?" Now I crawled all the way over and leaned against him.

He nodded, pulling me in. His muscles were tense as he kissed my head. "This really pushed yer da over the edge. He didn't want yer ma worryin' about some curse comin' after their daughter. He was already lookin' for work wit' his brother in Chicago at this point. He wanted ta get ya both away from yer gran's superstitions." Declan's hand brushed the journal just beneath his thigh. The disquiet on his face quickened my heartbeats. "Yer da wrote somet'in' about yer great-gran. She, uh—killed herself."

My mouth fell open. "What?"

"T'rew herself over the cliff, t'inkin' it would break the curse."

I gripped Declan's arm as the fingers of my family's bane

crawled up my spin. I didn't want to hear anymore, but this was also the most useful information so far.

Declan laid his hand over mine. "The story goes that yer great-gran didn't want to go t'rough wit' the curse she and her friend had whipped up against yer great-grandad. Turns out Landan was right about the witchcraft. But, anyway, that didn't work out so well for yer great-gran, as her witch friend said it was too late. She'd said somet'in' about yer great-gran's blood makin' the curse stick no matter what, and that if she didn't go t'rough wit' it, it would come back on her—and her daughter's, daughter's daughter."

"So, she killed herself?" I covered my mouth.

"That is what yer da wrote. Quite reluctantly too. He seemed ta be spittin' fire ta even write it. Almost like he was only recordin' it so he could show yer ma how daft it was later."

I whispered, "Her daughter's, daughter's daughter?" I rubbed my shaking palm against my forehead. "Dec, that's me. I'm the daughter."

Declan's throat flushed red again. "I know."

I shook my head, staring at my lap. "Is that all of it, then?"

"I'm afraid not. Yer da also said that yer gran had an older brother who died—at seventeen."

"My gran had mentioned she'd had a brother." I peered up at Declan. "What does he have to do with all this?"

"It had somet'in' ta do wit' yer great-grandad, and his death pushin' yer great-gran over the edge. No specifics as ta what happened to him, though."

"Oh." My insides twisted over the shocking reality of my family's history. How did any of this help me? Especially right now—trapped—with Balor possibly at our door. Or, up the stairs.

"When yer gran died, yer da was hopin' all this curse stuff would just go away, but then yer ma started hearin' the wind call her name. She was losin' her mind. Yer da didn't believe her—that it was all the t'ings yer gran had stuffed into her head. But then, he heard it too. Not only yer ma's name, but they were both hearin' *your* name too."

"My name?"

We paused, listening for the wind outside.

Nothing.

Declan squeezed me tighter. "That incident where we almost drowned in the cave happened just after that. I guess my da hadn't kept it quiet—he told yer da what'd happened. Yer ma was sure you were goin' ta die."

Heat surged into my cheeks. The memory of the horror-filled nights I used to spend in my bed as a child suddenly felt less like my imagination. Maybe there was a reason I'd been afraid of my bedroom windows.

I stuttered as I asked, "Th-then what?"

"Then, that's it. That is all he wrote. Seems ta me, though, that yer da might've snatched ya and yer ma away for a good reason."

"No," I almost yelled, tears welling in my eyes.

Declan caressed my cheek, guiding me against his chest. "Not sure if any of that helped, but—seems like we might've needed ta know it."

I didn't want to know *any* of it. Somehow my great-gran's witchcraft had been a nail in my coffin. The revelation that my dad may have moved us to Chicago to keep us safe was an onslaught of needles, pricking me with guilt—pushing me to think maybe I'd been wrong.

No. I don't believe it.

My anger toward my dad had been justified over the years. To think anything different would crumble my framework, just like Declan's rock towers.

"Nora?"

I gasped. "What?"

"Did ya . . . did ya know what yer gran's brother's name was?"

I shook my head. I may have heard it before, but I couldn't remember it now. "What was it?"

"His name was Lani."

"Lani?"

Sounds like Landan!

19

Witchcraft

"In order for it ta work, ya must get all the bones together," said a woman with long, dark hair tied back in a bun that rested against her neck. A few sparse hairs hung around her face. "We will need it all if we're ta heap yer husband's own guilt upon his head." Shadows danced over her striking blue eyes in the dark candlelight. "Yer blood will bind it."

"That's all," I said, hearing the sound of my voice. It was unusual. Not my own.

"The *magic* of the druids has a price, Moira."

Moira! That's my great-gran's name.

"What's the price?" I asked.

"Blood curses cannot be undone," the woman continued, a warning in her eyes. "The price comes back onto the witch who insights them if broken. It will be quite the gruesome task to acquire the elements we'll be needin'. Ya sure yer up for it?"

Hate boiled beneath my skin. "I won't be backin' down from this. He deserves whatever comes ta him."

The candle blew out with an exhaling breath. I was in darkness. The moon above me. My eyes adjusted, and I was now alone outside. Dirt smudged my hands and was crammed beneath my nails. My own tears trembled in my ears. Wind swished hair across my face.

Where am I?

Leaves rustled in tree limbs above me. Within the blue darkness, black silhouettes of crosses stood in rows along with what appeared to be gravestones. A cold stone church rose up on my right.

Am I in a graveyard?

My hands shook. Turned up soil lay before me, and . . . bones. Bones with gray flesh and decaying tissue still clinging to them. They were human ribs.

A scream echoed through my mind. The cawing of a crow harmonized with the high-pitched wail, making my blood run cold. I flung my hands over my ears.

The scene shifted. I was now in a room, folding something together into a thick canvas. The sobbing tears remained a cadence in my ears. The rib bones were there—a small skull, and a dismembered, feathered black wing.

The skull wasn't human. Too tiny—too delicate. The teeth were sharp like an animal's. A sinking feeling warned me that deep wickedness lingered on every element before me. The off-white cloth folded them together. Blood pooled in my palm, and I smeared it over the fabric.

NO!

I wished I could shout it out loud, but instead the voice of the other woman hissed into my ear, "It's in the blood."

I shut my eyes.

No more.

I was in front of The Flaherty House when I opened my eyes. Only it looked . . . different. It wasn't as white, and there was no driveway. Long grass waved in the night wind. A lantern was alight in my grandparents' bedroom window. Regret surged in my throat. Moira's thoughts were my own.

I don't want to curse him anymore. I don't want my husband to pay. Not like this.

Panic pummeled my chest. I whipped myself around and stared at the edge of the cliff. A green light pulsed out beyond the sea. The air grew heavier, pressing against my ribs with a nefarious buzz. It came closer—over the horizon.

A wicked cackle dripped into my ears like hot oil—horror stung my soul. "Your daughter's, daughter's daughter will be *cursed*. It's in the *blood*."

My legs started to run. The precipice loomed closer and closer, but I didn't stop. I leapt into the void, the icy wind biting at my skin as the raw terror of falling consumed every part of me.

"I WANT TO LIVE!" I screamed.

A crawling growl infiltrated my own voice. "It's in YOUR BLOOD."

I woke up screaming on the living room floor, my arms flailing. Declan was above me, holding my arms still.

"Yer dreamin', Nora! It's okay. It's okay."

Tears filled my eyes as I sat up, my hands covering my face. The words, *"It's in your blood,"* still reverberated in my head. I tried to shake off the nausea of free-falling.

It wasn't just a dream. It wasn't.

I couldn't breathe. I reached for Declan, and he pulled me into an embrace.

"It's okay," he said, but I was crumbling into pieces like burning peat in a fire.

"I don't want to die."

"Nora!" Declan's stern command was like a sobering slap. He pulled me back, and my eyes locked onto his. They kindled with a strength I'd never seen before. "Ya got ta snap out of this. Okay?"

I couldn't speak.

"Yer not goin' ta die. I'm not goin' ta let ya . . . and neither are you. Do ya hear me?"

I sniffed in my tears and sat up straighter.

"We have a busy day figurin' this all out. We can't do that if yer fallin' apart. Right?" He nodded, cupping my cheeks in his hands.

I returned his nod.

"Right, then." He moved to his feet and helped me up. I peered down at the small corner of the floor where we'd both fallen asleep next to the fireplace. I whimpered, wiping my sleeve cuff across my cheeks.

"There. I know ya, Nora. Yer a fighter. It isn't goin' ta do anythin' for ya ta fret like this, anyway." He breathed a heavy sigh, and his shoulders relaxed. "Scared the life out of me. Was it a nightmare?"

I nodded.

"Come on." He took my hand and pulled me into the dining room. He slid out a chair and escorted me to a seat. I stared at the shattered rusty box in front of me as Declan wandered into the kitchen. The rustle of plastic and the click of the toaster drew my attention. Declan seemed burdened as he stared out the window above the sink. His hair was a mess—falling over his eyes like it had when he was a kid. His gray T-shirt hung disheveled under his charcoal knitted jumper. But he kept moving forward—filling the kettle and preparing the mugs for tea.

Did he even get any sleep? Probably not.

I'd drifted off, leaning against his side while we tried to figure out what to do. Declan likely kept guard.

"Are the doors still locked?" I asked.

He nodded. "Thick fog outside still too, and no service on the phones." His eyes glared out the window. "I stayed up most of the night t'inkin'."

"Come up with anything?"

"Maybe." He turned to face me when the toaster popped,

catching his attention. I hid my relief with a shallow sigh. My mind was in a daze, unready to start making plans just yet.

I focused back on the eroded tin box. It looked like an empty shell with shattered pieces.

There isn't anything more in this box, is there?

Declan placed a freshly buttered piece of toast in front of me. "Eat."

I curled my lip. I didn't have much of an appetite.

"Eat, Nora."

I obeyed, taking a bite of the toast.

"No jam?"

"Sorry. No jam," he groaned, returning with a cup of tea. "It'll help yer head."

I touched the bump at the back of my skull and winced. Still sore.

"Do ya want ta talk about it?"

I grimaced. My head still swam from the morning dross and the trauma of . . . *everything.*

"The nightmare."

A lump in my throat made it difficult to swallow the bite of bread. I squeezed my wrist as if it would stop my cursed blood from pumping. The nightmare was too awful. I didn't want to discuss it just yet. Maybe if I didn't, it would fade away like some dreams do once fully awake.

Not this nightmare. I know better than that.

Some part of me still expected to hit the rocks at the bottom of the cliff. My teeth clenched, and I searched for a distraction.

My morning voice croaked, "Was there nothing in the box?"

Declan shook his head. "There really wasn't a moment ta tell ya about it last night. It, em . . . had a lot of sand in it. Tried ta see if there was anythin' of note in the sand, but I t'ink whatever's been inside it was eatin' away a long time ago."

I picked up one of the rusted bits. Seemed such a waste to

have gone to the cave now. I'd carried that thing all the way back, like a guilty weight cuffed to my arms—and for nothing.

"I'd hoped it was my Aunt Nieve's box."

"I thought of that. It might've been. There are a few pieces that look like they could've been coins." Declan joined me at the table, and we sat there in silence eating our toast and drinking our tea. He glanced at the hallway door.

"All my things are on the other side of that door."

"I know," Declan grumbled, sipping down the last of his tea and clunking his mug back onto the table. He pointed at the doorway with a daring smirk. "I'm going ta open that door. See what damage has been done."

"Right now?"

"I don't want ta be here longer than we have ta."

I couldn't argue with that.

"There may be a way out t'rough one of these windows. The fog won't come after me."

My mouth parted, and my eyes widened.

"I'm not goin' ta leave ya here, Nora." He huffed, rolling his eyes. "I'm just hopin' this fog will lift. It's still early. But as long as we're here, I am goin' ta make it safer." He pointed at the ceiling. "The window upstairs is probably broke. There's some wood in the shed. I could get it and board the windows up there. Probably should've done that before."

"It's not like you believed there was any sluagh before."

"True.' He nodded, still staring at the ceiling. "But I don't t'ink it would be good ta leave it open now. There's no wind. Should be safe. It's day—and t'ings are quiet."

"Not sure it—whatever it is—waits for night time."

"Probably right, but"—he scrunched his face—"it doesn't really feel like there is any threat right now, does it?"

I shrugged. "Not sure I want you going out in the fog either."

"It's fine, Nora. It's not comin' for me."

"We could both crawl out my grandparents' window. I think it slides open all the way. Then, we make a dash for the car together."

"Thought of that." He lifted his chin, worry lines etching his brow. "And we *will* do that, but . . . let's give the fog a chance ta clear. If the sluagh are out there, I'm not sure how ta protect ya. If it's just Irish weather—it will clear. Then we could leave."

"What about the doors?"

"We'd be using the windows, remember?"

"I know . . . What I mean is that the doors are still locked—the mobile phones . . . isn't that a sign that we aren't in the clear? That it isn't just"—I held up my fingers, making air quotations—"Irish weather." I shook my head and dropped it into my hands. "I can't believe this is happening."

Declan touched my arm. "Me either. But I refuse to sit here and do nothin' about it."

Declan offered his open palm to me. I folded my fingers between his, and he rubbed the back of my hand with his thumb. "I'm gettin' us out of this house. But, let's just give it a short while with the fog. Seems this curse ebbs and flows." He touched the rosary on my wrist. "Maybe some prayers for sunshine might work?"

Doing something—*anything*—was a good distraction. I needed one. The hope in Declan's eyes helped me to feel brave. "You're right. Let's open the hallway door. It's better than sitting here being afraid."

"A'right," Declan said, slapping the table and standing to his feet. "I'm opening that door." He moved over to the couch and slid it away from the door.

"How's your arm?"

"Achin'," he groaned, rolling his shoulder. "Nothin' serious, though. That damned bogeyman was right strong. Good t'ing I'm stronger." He winked, flashing a smile.

"Yeah, right." I smirked, rolling my eyes. The doldrums of my heaviness lifted ever so slightly.

That's the magic of Declan.

He gasped at the door. "Will ya look at that crack?" He ran his hand over the splintering line that threatened to break the door in two. His eyes shrank. The bolstered confidence from just a moment ago dwindled. He flicked the lock anyway.

Cautious anticipation rose in me as I leaned closer.

The doorknob wobbled in Declan's hand. "That will need to be fixed," he said with a throaty laugh.

I held my breath as he drew the door open and peered through the other side.

I gaped down the hallway. One half of the stairway door hung crooked on its hinges, while the other half lay on the floor.

Declan whistled, taking cautious steps into the hallway and peeking into each room before returning to the stairwell door. He propped the broken piece up against the wall. "Nothin' else seems disrupted."

I peered into my grandparents' bedroom. The curtains were wide open. The white fog on the other side was like a hollow eye threatening me. I didn't want to look at it. I didn't want it to see me. But I stared anyway, horror twisting my gut. My fingers curled, as if eager to reach the knob and pull the door shut. The need to crawl out that window grew less and less appealing.

"Shut the door," I whispered.

Declan's hands were on the handle in an instant, pulling the door shut.

I released my held breath. "Y-Yer right. It's foggy. I don't want to go out there yet."

The wind's faint whistle filtered down the stairs, stealing our attention. Declan gave me a warning look. "I'm goin' up there. Check t'ings out. You stay here."

"N-No. Declan, I—"

"I'll be fine, Nora. It isn't comin' for me anyway. Remember?"

"Why are you doing this?" I sort of snapped. "You could just leave. You could crawl out that window and never come back."

"Stop it, Nora. I don't need ya ta protect me. Besides— shouldn't have ta tell ya why I'm stickin' around. Wouldn't leave now even if ya asked me ta. Not unless yer comin' wit' me."

I couldn't go out there. Not yet.

The fog will clear.

I folded my arms, trying to hold onto what little bravery I had left. But I couldn't hold onto Declan as he crept up the stairs. My arms unwrapped, and I pulled at my sleeves instead. He hesitated at the top, his profile turned toward the bedroom.

"Is it all right?"

He held up his hand. "It's a'right, Nora. Just a mess."

My jaw tightened as he disappeared down the hall. Glass crackled beneath his footsteps. I breathed faster as I waited. It felt like an eternity when Declan appeared back over the top of the stairs. I exhaled, loosening my hold on my sweatshirt as he made his way down.

"Glass everywhere," he said, making it to the bottom.

"Is that it?"

"Yah." He nodded. "The windows are broke, glass all over the bed and the floor, but nothin' else. I'll clean it up and get the windows boarded up. That is if I can find a way ta get out ta the shed and bring in some boards. Otherwise, I might have ta use what I can find in the house." He stroked his chin. "It would be good if I could find some cardboard too."

"I can help." Anything was better than being alone *anywhere* in this house. Even upstairs.

He stared at me for a second as though considering.

The creak of an opening door groaned from the kitchen. I

grabbed Declan's arms. He looked behind me toward the noise. He held his finger to his lips. "Stay here."

Wait. Isn't this the dangerous side of the house?

I clung to his arm, refusing to let go.

He flicked his chin for me to follow. We crept down the hallway and peeked past the door. Declan stood taller, taking a step back.

"What is it?"

He pointed. The kitchen door hung wide open. The white fog whirled outside, calling my doom with its silence.

20

More Secrets

eclan appeared at the bottom of the stairs, collecting planks from a pile of two-by-fours he'd brought in. He had survived a few treks to the shed but still didn't think it was safe for me to go out there. To him, the open kitchen door seemed like a nefarious invitation into the monster's jaws. We weren't free. Boarding the windows was the most effective plan. For now, at least, it kept us busy.

"How's it going?"

"Took forever ta get the glass cleaned up. Still not sure I got it all." Declan glanced up the stairwell. "Not even sure it matters." He turned toward me, and his distressed face melted into a smile. "Some sun is peekin' t'rough the haze. There hasn't been any wind. We might be able ta leave soon." The promise in his words and the warmth of his sea-green eyes calmed me. His fingers tugged a ringlet next to my face, then he leaned in for a kiss.

His lips brushed mine in a simple sweet peck, and I wished that was all it took to magically break my curse right then and there—just like in the fairy tales. He probably wanted to be the knight that stole me away from my grandmother's curse. I wanted that too—with all my being.

Declan had always been just right for me. Not sure why it took me so long to see it. His smile was like a lighthouse. His lash rimmed eyes, the shining lantern calling the lost ship of my heart back to shore. It was more than a simple grin. There was something there, in who he was, that had always been a part of me. He'd been with me through everything. He was my beacon in every storm.

Storm.

Unease returned as I forced a smile. How could I keep him from being stolen away? His soft eyes weren't without anxiety either. The longer he looked at me, the more the corners of his mouth sank.

"I'm scared," I said, my lips trembling.

His brows pinched. "Me too." Declan stroked my cheek, searching my eyes as though an answer to my fear lay inside them. "Listen," he said, "we aren't going ta just wait this out and shake in our boots. That's what yer ma and gran did. And, I t'ink ya may be right—runnin' won't save ya. Not for long, anyway. The women in yer family—"

"What?"

He sighed. "I don't mean ta be bold, but ya aren't like them. It's like they just accepted their fate and let it come take them. Yer gran bantered on in warning about the curse until the day she died, but she did *nothin'*. If Landan says there is somet'in' ta be done about this, then there is a way. Yer family has just turned a blind eye ta it. I'm not goin' ta do that. Are you?"

Hope kindled in my chest. "You're putting some fight in me."

"The fight was already there."

"No." I shook my head. "Apparently, I run." Disappointment in my behavior squeezed my chest. "You're my fight, Dec. Always have been."

His eyes brightened, and a smile lit his face. The honesty in my confession bridged the gap between us. He rushed in for another kiss, deeper and more passionate than before. His hands slid down the curve of my back, pulling me closer. His height tipped me back, but I was safe in his embrace. A fire ignited inside me, a desirous flame I didn't want to extinguish, but all too soon, he broke the kiss and pulled his face away.

For the first time, he looked at me with an unguarded truth in his eyes—no more barriers or hidden feelings.

"Good," he uttered. "I'm glad if I've given ya fight. But—I'm not the one who jumped on that airplane, or blazed back down ta that cave as though it were nothin'. There's gumption in ya. Maybe that's why it will be different for you than it was for them." He let go, shaking his head as if reluctant to release me, then picked up several boards. "Ya comin'? It's safe. Doesn't appear Balor likes the mornin' sunshine peekin'. No wind, either."

"Yeah," I said, still beaming from his kiss. New hope lifted me, and I scrambled up the stairs behind Declan.

He'd taped cardboard over the windows. I breathed easier without the open windows yawning threats at me. Declan had pushed the bed to the side so he could maneuver easier and complete his task.

Declan stuck a few nails in his mouth, then lifted the first board into place at the bottom of the window. He flicked his head toward the board. "Ya want ta help me hold this?"

I rushed over and held it level.

Declan winked, pulling the first nail from his lips, and hammered it into the left side of the board. "One more ought to do the trick." He pounded another nail in. "Okay, ya can let go."

I stood back as he finished hammering the rest of the nails into the other side. We repeated the process until three boards covered the windows—a small gap remained along the top that still needed to be covered. The boundary between us and Balor seemed more solidified. Whether it truly created safety or not, it helped me forget the curse, if only for a moment. A slow smile tugged at my lips as Declan's back muscles flexed beneath his half-untucked T-shirt while he worked.

"Two more boards ought ta do it." He stood back from the window, placing his hands on his hips. "Gotta couple more down the stairs. I'll get them."

He dashed away like a man on a mission, leaving me behind to scan the room. With each passing moment, this space became more and more a place of my past. Less familiar. A place I didn't want to stay. Even the treasures I'd gathered from the boxes held less value to me now: one of my gran's figurines, a pink flowery teacup from her china collection, some of my favorite books, a teardrop pendant my mother used to wear— among other things. But I would still take them when we were all finished, along with my suitcase, and stow them in the boot of Declan's car—once the threat had passed and the sun shone. It seemed like it would happen. The doors were unlocked and the threat of fog slowly melted away.

This house was just an echo from my past that didn't hold what I thought it would. I'd found what I was looking for. A person who still lived and breathed—not just shadowy remnants of a past life I once had.

I started gathering the things from the bed to take downstairs. I peered toward a boarded window, and my eye caught something just beneath it—a white board that didn't match the rest of the wood-paneled wall. It had been nailed in, just like Declan's boards above. Curiosity pulled me toward it. Could've just been a repair to the wall done poorly, but at this point, I had to get a closer look. I knelt in front of the board and pried at the wood with the tips of my fingers.

"Whatcha doin'?" Delcan asked, two more boards in tow.

"Check this out." I pointed to a rectangular patch. "What do you think this is?"

"A really bad patch job."

I giggled as he set the boards down and knelt beside me. "That's what I was thinking. But then, I thought—"

"Ya want to see if there is anything behind it."

I nodded.

"All right. Let's see." He took the back end of the hammer and started prying it off the wall. The nails croaked against the old wood as Declan worked them free. He tore the piece from the wall, and then we peered inside.

Old webs clung to the framework, mixed with crumbling plaster. But tucked just beneath the interior framework was a roll of dusty fabric. Butterflies swarmed into my stomach.

"Ya want me ta get it?" he asked.

"Sure." My body trembled. Fear closed around my throat as he pulled the suspicious, stained-off-white bundle free. "I know what this is."

Declan tried to hand it to me, but I shook my head. He must have noticed the fright eking from my eyes. He placed it on the floor.

"What is it?" he asked.

"This is it." I reached for his arm, clenching his sleeve in my fist. "My gran's curse."

His eyes widened. "What do ya mean?"

"My nightmare—last night. I don't think it was just a dream. I saw what my great-gran and her witch friend did."

"Should I put it back?"

I shook my head. "Maybe we should burn it."

"What's inside?"

I gulped, dreading the contents, yet compelled to unveil them and confirm I wasn't losing my mind. My fingers reached for the twine that bound the parcel. The old stains, now brown, was my great-gran's blood. I undid the knot and unrolled the fabric. Decayed remnants unfurled. My heart thundered as if it might burst from my chest.

Declan jerked his sleeve over his mouth and nose. "Are those bones?"

The small skull was cracked in two pieces. The feathered wing was like a dusty old taxidermy. The rib bones were brittle—lined with cracks.

"Is that a cat skull?" Declan recoiled, scrunching his face.

"I think my great-gran put this here."

"This is *the* witchcraft?"

My gut wrenched tighter than a vise. "I think so."

"No wonder this room is where the t'ing wants ta come t'rough."

That revelation struck a chord in my chest.

"We're most definitely burnin' this," Declan said, rising to his feet. "Don't touch it. I'll get a bag."

Yes. Burn it. Maybe this could set me free?

Declan bolted away. I stared at the wicked pile and shuddered.

What could have possibly caused my great-gran to do this?

21

One Last Look

"Here," Declan said, helping me situate my arms through the backpack. His eyes scanned the sky as he sighed. "Everything is clear. Almost like there was never any threat."

"Like all the chaos was all just in our heads." I rolled my eyes. "Once the sun is shining, it always makes me question everything I thought I saw."

Declan's jaw tightens. "Well, it wasn't in our heads and"—he gazed toward the horizon—"the sun will be sinkin' soon. We need ta get goin'."

I nodded, cinching the straps over my shoulders, while Declan tossed a large bag of kindling and peat over his. "Feels weird having that *thing* in my backpack."

"We can't burn those bones soon enough."

"I think it was a good idea not to burn it in the house." I shuddered, thinking about the sluagh's wind snuffing out any fire we attempted to make.

"Ya, I'd a bad feelin' about doin' it there. Like somet'in might happen. Feels safer being away from that house."

I peered over my shoulder. I couldn't get enough distance between myself and the house. Declan's pinched expression suggested he felt the same way. The beach was the best place to rid ourselves of Great-Gran's cursed bundle. There was a fire pit that Declan and I used to use near our secret fort. The flames of the pit already burned in my stomach, anxious to discover if this was all it would take to set me free and break the curse.

"Come on." Declan indicated with his chin, and we moved toward the path to the beach.

I scrambled behind Declan, peering over my shoulder as if the cursed spirits would follow us from the house. At least the call of the flailing curtains from the open upstairs window had been silenced. Only brown cardboard showed through the broken glass of the windowpanes. But now I carried the curse with me. A sickening pulse disrupted my heart beat every time I remembered its presence against my back.

Declan assisted me down the ledge that led to the trail. I couldn't wait for the house to disappear. Our scampering feet leapt and pivoted down the trail until the rock stairs slowed our pace.

Declan's movements were more delicate with his heavy load. His long legs gave him the advantage, while I had to shimmy down each step.

I breathed a long sigh as I leapt off the final ledge onto the shore's sandy pebbles. I smiled at Declan as though I was an escaped convict who had finally cleared the sight of the prison guards and was homefree. I folded my fingers into Declan's hand. A warm grin lit his face.

He lifted my hand to his lips. "I got ya, Nora Morrigan. We're goin' ta get this finished. I promise."

Something about the hopeful anticipation in his gaze helped me believe him. Memories kindled of how excited I used to be waiting for Declan after school on the beach when we were kids. I would shed my uniform jumper and throw rocks in the sea to pass the time until he came. Sometimes I'd find a sharp piece of rock and carve pictures into the driftwood.

Doubt any of my old graffiti remains.

We almost never missed a day. Sometimes I would even wait in town, near the post office, to head Declan off. It always seemed like I didn't have to wait as long for him if I met him there.

"What would your parents think about the two of us together like this? I mean, like"—heat rushed into my face—"you and me, going out together."

"Well," he said with a chuckle, pulling me along toward our old fort, "me shiftin' wit' a troublemaker again might make them t'ink I've traded in my halo."

I gasped, smacking his arm.

"Nah. Ya know how much they love ya. Probably more t'rilled than Della will be. But ya know who will be over the moon, might even be more than we can handle, is Carla. Her and Don have been talkin' for years how much they t'ought the two of us were meant ta be together."

"Really?" I blushed.

"Ya know that they love ya, Nora. Come on now." He nudged my arm with his elbow. "Once Carla knows, she won't be able ta leave ya alone over it."

I squeezed his hand, but a surge of sadness hit me hard—like something wedged in my ribs—and I shifted. "I just wish I knew what was going to happen."

"Me too. Do ya t'ink burnin' that unholy bundle of bones will break the curse?"

"It's worth a try." I tracked my blue shoes as they scuttled through the pebbles. "What if this is my last look at the sea? What if this is the last time you and I—"

"Nora—"

"I don't want it to be my last. I'm going to do everything I can to make sure that it isn't. It just—it feels so desperate. It's real, Declan." I let go of his hand and fingered the rosary beads at my wrist.

What was that prayer Gran used to always pray? Hail Mary, full of grace, the Lord is with thee . . .

Declan wanted me to have hope, and I did, but there was

also part of me that couldn't help but fear the worst. If I failed to fight hard enough, would it all end today—tomorrow—the next day? When would death's scythe tear through my soul?

"Ya just . . . can't talk like that if we are going ta beat this."

My eyes trailed behind me to the house. I rolled my shoulders beneath the backpack straps. That *cursed thing* was too close to me.

"We're on our way to burn it. And just like we planned, we'll go from there—try ta find Landan."

I nodded. "If Landan really wants to help—he'll find us."

"Seems like he always comes when I'm not around, though."

"That's not what happened last night."

"Either way. I'm not leavin' ya." He paused. "Hey?"

I lifted my gaze to meet his green quavering eyes. They held the same sinking dread that slithered through my bones.

"Don't give *it* the satisfaction of yer fear."

"How can I not?" I flung my hands, my footfalls growing heavier.

"I don't know. I just keep t'inkin' we got ta do t'ings different. My years of bein' a footballer in school showed me that the game was mostly in how well ya intimidated yer enemy, right? If my team started t'inkin' we were cornered, then the other team would dominate us. Yer gran and yer ma sounded like they were afraid."

"How do you not fear a monster that wants to take your life?"

He put up his hands as if asking me to hear him out. "How do they coach ya in track?"

"Endurance. Mind over matter."

"Well, ya know how ta do it then."

"This isn't a sport—or a game."

"I know. Sorry." Declan dropped his head. "Just tryin' ta t'ink of anythin' I can. My da calls me a problem solver. It gets under me ma's skin."

"I'm glad you're like that." I squeezed his sleeve. "Not sure what I'd do if you weren't."

"Ya know." His breath clipped, and he stopped his traipse and turned toward the waves. Tears formed in the bottom of his eyes. "I t'ought about ya almost every day. And yer the same. The same Nora who made me laugh, and always got me inta trouble." He paused, biting his bottom lip. "And here we are inta so much trouble." He swiped a tear before it could fall. "I don't want ta be in this situation, Nora. But, I also want ta have ya wit' me. I'll do whatever it takes."

My eyes moistened, and I sucked in my cheeks, holding the emotions in as tightly as I could.

He kicked at the pebbles beneath his feet, then paused. He bent down and collected a whelk shell from the pebbles. His face softened and his brows lifted as he gazed at it. "Remember how I made ya a bracelet wit' one of these once a long time ago?"

I nodded, huffing a small laugh. Two tears escaped.

I can't believe he remembers that. I loved it so much.

I cleared my throat. "I lost it that day in the cave when we almost drowned."

He pressed his lips together and nodded. "We are putting t'ings right now. No'ting else is goin' ta be stolen from us. Not anymore." He handed me the shell. "I promise." He tucked it into my palm and folded his hands around mine. "Maybe it's daft, but—"His eyes shone with clarity. "T'ings like this matter."

A sweet wave of completion stole my voice. "It's . . . not . . . daft." This small, white shell was one of the things that had been stolen away. Now it had been given back, like the sun had after our dark, foreboding night.

"Come on. Let's get this done." He squeezed my hand a little tighter before letting go.

I followed him, rolling my fingers over the ridges of the

shell as if it symbolized the end of my nightmare, and then slipped it into my pocket.

"Here it is." Declan kicked at the stones surrounding the fire pit. It was tucked away from the shoreline, closer to the inland rocks, in a cove where our old fort used to be. "Still come here sometimes when I want a fire."

Declan shrugged off the large bag from his shoulder and started unloading the peat and dry wood. I unslung my backpack and unzipped it. The plastic crinkled as I removed the black trash bag that contained the cursed bones.

"Shouldn't take long ta get a fire blazin'."

I peered down at the bag, and a shiver snaked through me. If only hurling it into the sea would do the trick. Instead, I had to hold it until the fire was ready. "Make sure the fire is big."

"Yah—can't have any of those bones missin' the flames. That's why I made sure to bring enough fuel, and this." He held up a can of lighter fluid and shook it. The liquid sloshed in the tin.

The wind chill bit around my neck. I cinched my jacket tighter.

Declan built a teepee of wood around a pile of peat, then sprayed it with lighter fluid. The pungent gas wafted into my nose. I always liked the smell. It cued memories of fires with Declan and the taste of the barbeque dinners we used to have with his family.

The click of Declan's lighter ignited a tiny flame on the wood. The blue line of fire swept over the fuel before it sparked with orange flames. I stepped closer to Declan as the crackling wood caught, and warmth radiated against my cold cheeks.

"Once we get some of those hot coals formin', we'll toss the bones in."

I grabbed Declan's arm, leaned into him, and he wrapped his arm around me. His warmth rivaled any flame. For a moment, the world beyond the firelight didn't matter, as though we were here for no other purpose than to share an evening together.

My coiled nerves loosened. I was on the cusp of ridding myself of my great-gran's pestilence. I wanted to believe that burning it would be enough, and I would be free. I even dared to imagine Declan and I walking away from the shore, hand in hand. The curse behind me. My mother's death avenged. I could then grieve the loss differently after this.

The sea was calm. The seagulls soared overhead, hunting for morsels in the abating waves. The sun dipped into the dark blue horizon.

Declan kissed the top of my head. "I t'ink the fires burnin' good enough. Let's be rid of it."

I stepped toward the fire and lifted the bag above it—eager for the flames to consume it.

"DON'T BURN IT!" came a loud shout from the other side of the flames.

I jumped, and Declan stumbled back.

Landan held his hands out, his eyes wide. "Ya cannot burn it. Just—just put it down, Nora."

I froze. My arm still lifted the bag aloft.

"Ya have ta listen ta me," Landan urged. "Ya can't burn it yet."

"Throw it in," Declan yelled, taking several menacing steps toward Landan, his jaw muscles flexing.

Landan met the challenge, stepping closer to Declan. "Don't, Nora!" he warned, his eyes blazing at Declan. "Don't listen ta him. He doesn't know what will happen. What're ya even doin' here, Declan?"

Declan cocked his jaw. "Ya t'ink I'm goin' ta let her come here alone?"

"She doesn't need ya ta solve this."

"Oh"—Declan took another step forward—"but she needs you—the black cat that eats kibble on her doorstep—a shape-shiftin', deceitful gancanagh?"

Landan's lips twisted, and he balled his hands into fists. "Ya have no idea what I am."

"STOP!" I yelled, the arguing gnawing at my insides. My hand still gripped the bag, ready to let it go. "Stop it!" My body trembled.

If I burn the cursed parcel, will something worse happen? And if I don't, am I falling prey to a devil?

"How do I know if I can trust you, Landan? What even are you?"

<h1 style="text-align:center">22</h1>

The Gancanagh

Landan stretched his finger toward the bag. "Nora, if ya burn that now, I won't be able ta help ya."

"Why? You have to tell me *why*?" I implored him. "I want to live, Landan. I don't know that I can trust you. You aren't human."

He stood silent in the dusky light. The flames highlighted the shadow over his eyes. The wind ruffled through his unbuttoned peacoat. "I'm not what ya t'ink I am."

"Enough! Then what are you?" I asked, my voice pitchy. Desperation pulsed in my chest.

"It was Saoirse's meddlin' that stopped me from helpin' Nieve." Landan whipped his pointed finger toward Declan. "And now *he's* gettin' in the way."

Saoirse? That's Gran!

I faltered, nearly dropping the bag. I lowered it to my side. "Saoirse didn't trust me."

The plastic bag crinkled as I gripped it in both hands. "What are you, Landan? I can't trust you either if I don't know."

Declan cocked his head. "Are ya Lani?"

Landan's gaze snapped to Declan's, a storm simmering in his green eyes. "It isn't that simple."

"That simple?" Declan yelled. "Either yer the ghost of a dead son—or yer a demon."

The wind picked up, its icy gusts biting at my ears. Fear surged through my already tense body, and at any moment, the wind might howl my name. I inched closer to Declan.

Declan shot out his hand. "Stay by the fire, Nora!"

I froze. Anxiousness clashed like churning waves in my stomach—the urge to run a hammering impulse I couldn't shake.

Landan's teeth clenched. "Yer not gettin' in my way, Declan."

"I'm not goin' ta let ya hurt Nora."

Landan's gaze whipped toward the sea. His dark hair blew over his face, exposing the rippling tension in his jaw.

I followed his gaze to the sea. A billowing fog rolled in.

"Listen," Landan pleaded, turning back to face me. His brows now curved with worry. "I don't want ta scare ya, Nora, but there isn't time."

"Just tell me what I need to know," I insisted, my voice almost a scream.

"Fine!" His eyes flashed with the fire's reflection. "I am the curse that is in yer blood."

"What?" Heavy weight pressed on my chest, and my knees nearly buckled.

"Lani's rib bones are in that bag. I am him, but I'm also the blood that curses ya."

My fight retreated like a wave rolling back into the sea. "I-I don't know what that means. If you're Lani, then how come Gran and Aunt Neive didn't recognize you?"

"Has it escaped yer notice that I can change my form?" Black wings unfurled behind him.

I screamed, stumbling in the pebbled sand. The caw of crows infiltrated my ears.

"You're the sluagh that chased me!"

"No, I'm the crow that made ya run." He flung his hand toward the sea. His wings flickered as he moved. The fog barreled closer. A green tinge lit the oncoming clouds. "That is what ya keep calling the sluagh—or Balor. None of those names matter. It's just death, because of me Ma."

The world tipped sideways as though I was on a ship on a stormy sea—the unsteady deck rocking beneath my feet. Landan, the birds—the same? My sense of reason pushed back, refusing to believe it. "But you were Buttons?"

"Does it matter? I was there to protect ya every time. Shouldn't that be enough ta trust me?"

Declan took a lunging step toward Landan. "Yer also the one who has been there every time the chaos has come. We were fine here until ya showed up. Nora!" He jerked his head toward me. "Throw the bag into the fire!"

I clutched the bag to my chest. Declan dashed toward me. Landan's wingless form chased after him, but spectral black crows furled in his wake as he collided with Declan. Their bodies careened past me into the driftwood and rocks.

"Declan!" I screamed, scrambling to my feet.

Landan stood. Declan remained on the ground, unmoving. My heart stopped. A scream tore from my throat, and I crashed to my knees at his side. Declan's head lay against a stone. Blood dribbled from his temple onto the rock.

Declan!

Fear clogged my throat, stealing my voice. I reached for him, but Landan snatched my wrist and yanked me to my feet. I stared at Landan in a daze. The plastic bag slipped from my fingers, dropping at my feet. Landan spoke, but I couldn't register his words. My head buzzed. Despair sank its claws into my chest. I disappeared inside my mind, searching for a place to hide. Not from Landan. Not from the fog, but from the pain that sizzled my every sense.

Not Declan.

A moan crawled out of my throat. I pictured Declan in my mind. His kisses, the look in his eyes when he butterflied my chin, him splashing me in the sea when we were children—bright laughter lighting up his entire face.

"Nora!" Landan's voice filtered through the muteness of my trauma. I turned toward the sea. The fog hovered over the shore, inching its way closer.

"*N-O-R-A!*" the ever-pervading wind boomed into my ears.

I reached toward Declan, but Landan pulled me back. "There's no time. We have ta run."

Tears spilled out of my eyes. "I won't leave him!"

"I'm sorry, Nora. I didn't mean ta. He was goin' ta make t'ings worse, just like Saoirse."

I was dead inside. All hope of a future faded as I peered back at Declan's motionless form. He didn't move. The wind tousled his hair. His mouth gaped lifelessly. My stomach turned.

I'm going to throw up.

Landan's grip tightened around my wrist. My gran's rosary dug into my skin. I yelped, but that didn't stop him. He pulled me along the beach at a rapid pace. I tried to resist, but the rosary—it pinched deeper. He was too strong. I vomited upon the sandy pebbles, leaving a trail as Landan yanked me forward.

"Declan!" I screamed over and over again.

My feet scrambled to keep up. I tumbled forward onto my knees.

"Come on, Nora!" Landan hoisted me around the waist, carrying me over his shoulder like a bag of sand. The pebbles were a blur beneath Landan's feet. The voice of death groaned my name from the sea. The virescent glow permeated the fog that enveloped us.

Declan was supposed to be with me. Even if these were my final breaths, he would be there.

Landan's strides never slowed, and his breath never heaved. His urgency seemed to push him forward like someone who didn't require breath. Heat didn't radiate from his skin. He wasn't cold either. He just *was.*

Pebbles were no longer beneath us. I hung there, his shoulder digging into my swirling stomach as rock steps appeared. Then a trail. Then level ground.

I know where we are.

"No!" I screamed, fight returning to me.

Landan set my feet on the grassy turf.

The Flaherty House stood before me.

Landan grabbed me by the shoulders and leveled with my eyes. "Ya need ta break the curse, Nora. Not just for you, but for me too. Do ya t'ink I like bein' trapped like this—unable to stop me own kin from dyin', one after the other?"

My lips trembled, and tears swam in my vision. "Do you think I care about what happens to you after what you did to Declan?"

"I didn't mean ta. I just wanted ta keep him away from burnin' that curse."

Air billowed from my lungs, fueled with fire. "I am the last one, Landan! No one comes after me. You'll be free— FREE! You won't have to save anybody after me. There won't be anyone left to save. Just let me die!"

"I want ta save ya, Nora." He glanced over his shoulder. His eyes flared wider. "Come on. We need ta get inside."

"Why? What can we do in there that we can't do out here?"

"It'll give us time."

"Time to what?"

"Break the curse. *Please*," he urged. "Please let me help ya."

I couldn't stop the tears from flooding down my cheeks as I looked to where we'd left Declan. The beach was covered in the beryl fog. My chin trembled. Rage ransacked my sanity. I wished I could rip Landan to pieces.

"I'll never forgive you!" I shouted.

He stood back. His shoulders drooped, and the green in his eyes faded to gray. "That's the whole problem, isn't it?" His jaw tightened. "How *many* can ya begrudge before it eats ya alive?"

I coiled at the threat in his voice.

What does that even mean?

His lips straightened in a line. "Maybe yer right. There isn't any point. Good luck ta ya."

I gasped against a sob. The finality of Landan's tone struck me to my core. If he wasn't going to fight for me, there was no one left.

No answers.

No freedom.

I really would die.

He morphed into a cat before my eyes and scampered toward the house. The front door opened on its own, and he disappeared inside.

23

The Hard Way

My stomach dropped. Was I really going to stand here and let whatever comes get me?

Part of me longed to rush into the fog—come what may—all the way back to Declan. Was he even alive? We'd left him behind, bleeding. Maybe all he needed was a doctor. I choked on the lump rising in my throat and pinched the whelk shell in my pocket. The ache to have touched him before Landan pulled me away tore at my gut. My fingers dug into my stomach, and I doubled over. Blood rushed to my head, and a silent cry escaped my lips. Grief—blinding and suffocating—pressed on me like a crushing weight, driving me toward the ground.

Declan's face—the way it drooped over the stone—and I'd just left him there.

I thought of my mom too. Her hands caressing my face. Me waving goodbye through the car window the last time I saw her.

I'll never see Mom again. Maybe Declan either.

Anger swelled inside me. I clenched my hands into fists and screamed at the house. The roar erupted from deep within, pulling me upright. My temples throbbed as waves of rage rushed through me. I was a fighter now, but not the kind I wanted to be. Not the kind that Declan thought I was.

I stormed toward the house, pushing through the open door.

"Landan!"

I searched for him, my eyes adjusting to the darkness. Quiet whimpers stopped me cold. Their frail timbre flooded through my blood like ice, cooling my fury. The weeping came from the direction of the fireplace. I turned. Landan's shadowed figure lay curled on the floor, sobbing.

"What are you doing?" I snapped, clinging to my anger as a safety net.

"I'm sorry, Nora."

I stepped closer, hand outstretched toward him, but I pulled it back.

"I'm just as bad as *him*," Landan wailed.

The wind howled louder outside. My name echoed through the house in fleeting moans. I struggled to maintain the grip on my resolve.

"Please, Landan. Who?"

"My da."

I moved closer and knelt in front of him. I needed him. If he truly did want to help me, he was the only person who could. His pale face was clearer now. Tear lines glistened on his cheeks.

"I was seventeen. My da was drunk." Landan sniffed. "He was goin' ta hurt me ma. I couldn't let him hurt her. She didn't deserve that. I told Saoirse and Neive ta go upstairs. I didn't want them ta see their da like that." He shook his head into the crooks of his arms. "As if I could protect them."

I placed my hand on his knee. "Landan. Maybe you couldn't help then, but you can help now. The curse is coming, isn't it? I'm sorry I said what I did, but I need your help."

"My da started hitting her. I don't know what happened. I just snapped. I was so angry. I wanted ta save me ma from being hurt. I tried ta hit him. My da bein' drunk, I t'ought I'd have the upper hand, but he had rocks for fists. He hit me, and I fell."

"L-Landan, I need you to tell me what to do." The wind slammed into the house. I gulped. The monster would try to break in next. I grabbed the collar of his peacoat. "I need you to snap out of it."

"After he hit me, I fell. My head landed on the edge of the mantle." He focused his quivering eyes on mine. "I—I died."

I gasped, covering my mouth. "Great-Grandad was the one who killed you?"

"As I floated away from my body, I saw me da collapse beside me. He hadn't meant to do it. He was mourning what he'd done. Me ma was screamin' and beatin' her fists on his back. She'd never *forgive him*." His last words echoed in an eerie vibrato. His eyes locked with mine. They weren't green but a darkened gray. The front door suddenly slammed shut.

Landan burst to his feet—I fell back, catching myself with my hands. His wings manifested behind him and crawled like growing shadows across the walls.

"She *hated* him so much that a sickness blackened her soul," Landan growled, in the same dark voice that sounded more like the sluagh. "She became willing ta dig up my corpse and carve out my bones. Bitterness poisoned her marrow. She wanted me da ta pay."

Landan grew taller and taller. His wings enveloped the room. I scooted away from him until my back hit the couch. He now embodied the threat of Balor with his looming frame and soulless eyes. Outside, the cursed wind rattled against the loose windowpanes. The walls creaked and cracked at each crashing stroke.

Landan's inflection deepened. "Her sin is in yer blood, Nora Morrigan."

A deafening crash shook the house, and the floor quaked beneath me.

The house is going to tear apart!

I threw one arm over my head, curling the other into my chest. A sharp pain shot through my wrist. I extended my arm, wincing at the smarting sting. The struggle with Landan, when he pulled me across the beach, had driven the rosary into my skin.

Landan boomed, "My ma swore she'd never *forgive* me da. Saoirse and Neive despised him."

"But he did wrong!" I screamed above the mayhem. "Didn't he deserve their hate?"

Landan was suddenly in front of my face, gritting his teeth. He'd returned to the wingless Landan that I recognized, but his eyes—they were still gray. He grabbed my wrist with the rosary and squeezed. I screamed as blood dripped down my arm.

The noise. The pounding and crashing. The unrelenting cry of my name. *"N-O-R-A!"* All of it hammered my eardrums, overwhelming my senses.

Landan's face pulsed with rage. "And yer da? Does he deserve the poison of yer unforgiveness too?"

He doesn't understand what my dad's done—what he's put me through.

"And Una—yer ma hated her da because he was aloof and disconnected. Did he deserve it?" His eyes bore into mine. "Damn it, Nora! The curse claims ya like it has them all."

The words I yelled at my dad on our way to the airport echoed through my head:

"You let her die! You always have to control everything, except the things that matter—don't you? I don't need anything from you. And I certainly don't have anything left to give you."

The hurt in my dad's eyes kindled in my memory. He recoiled like a snake had bit him—like the breath had been stolen from his lungs.

I gasped.

Landan snarled. "Yer unforgiveness chews away at yer own bones. Yer blood festers with the poison."

Landan's words chiseled into me like an icepick.

I yanked my wrist free of his grip. The front window shattered, spraying glass shards into the house. Landan shielded me with his body. The force smashed me between him and the couch as it slid across the floor. My knees buckled, and I collapsed. My eyes fluttered. Landan's black wings wrapped around me as fog poured in from the window.

My consciousness faded. Viridescent light flickered like lightning.

Landan's voice reverberated in my head, "You can take the poison out. Nora! Don't stop fighting."

"W-Where am I?" I murmured, glancing around. The fog surrounded me, but it was white. I squinted, shielding my eyes against the bright daylight. The threat of darkness and curses had vanished.

I sat on my grandad's bench. Landan sat beside me, leaning with his elbows on his knees, staring into the blank fog.

"Landan?"

He faced me. His eyes were green, and the likeness of my old friend appeared in them again. He shot me a smile. *That* smile. The one he used to give me that made me feel like I was special—like he was special too.

"What're we doing here?"

"We need ta talk. And I'm here, same as I've always been, ta help ya."

I grinned, happy he was here, but then the smile fell from my face. "You keep saying that. But I don't understand what I am supposed to do. And you"—my lips twisted—"hurt, Declan. You hurt me."

Green light pulsed. My eyes locked onto the dark ceiling. Pain ripped through the veins in my arms.

I didn't escape. Is this what happened to Mom and Gran when they died?

The curse devoured me. My hope dashed like Declan's head on that rock. Surrender threatened to take me.

Landan stood with his dark wings unfurled.

My neck strained and my teeth clenched, I yelled, "Help me!"

Landan remained unmoved like a pitiless statue.

The light flickered again.

"We don't have a lot of time, Nora."

My brows furrowed. "I know."

"This is all the time I've left ta tell ya what ya need ta know."

"Are you the one hurting me—right now, in my gran's house?" My voice trembled—I refused to believe it was him. He'd been my friend. But, out there, in the real world, my body was breaking—and he was there, watching, doing nothing to help me.

His lips thinned, and he dropped his head. "Part of me is. The other part is trying ta save ya."

How is that possible?

This place was unusual. We were somewhere in my subconscious. Landan didn't frighten me here. All the chaos was silenced, and I could think. Listen. "Are you the curse that's come for me?"

"No, but I'm part of it—as are you. This rage—this

anger—this has all come from Moira and her daughters. Every life has only added to the furor."

Landan's words aligned in the calm, bright atmosphere—free from noise, fear, or chaos.

I looked down at my hands. "It's hate. Isn't it?"

Landan smiled. He reached for my hand and turned it over, revealing my gran's rosary around my wrist.

I rubbed the cross between my fingers. "What do I have to do to break it?"

"You have ta start wit' yerself."

I worked my jaw, loathing to admit the truth. "I've hated my dad."

Landan's hand wrapped around mine. "What can be done about that?"

"I could—forgive him."

"Can ya do that, Nora?"

Remorse swirled in my chest. I'd blamed my dad for everything for so long. All my pain had been his fault. Always.

Can I let go of that?

"Yer life depends on it."

Green light struck again. Windows in the kitchen burst. Glass scattered across the floor. Aching pain rolled through my arms like fingers clawing toward my heart, snatching away my breath. Landan leapt over me, his mouth transforming into a hideous black beak. Inky feathers sprawled like a crown encircling his head. He cawed a terrifying shriek in my face—a warning call. The same as the one he crowed that day I fell off the cliff.

Snap out of it and fight.

I drew a deep breath. "I forgive you." I sobbed, turning my head away from Landan's terrifying bird-like, black eyes. "I forgive you, Dad!" Tears dripped from my eyes. I tried to roll away from Landan, but he held me fast. Roots of pain that dug through my veins toward my chest suddenly unraveled like a taut rope being cut. I could breathe.

Landan's pale features surfaced once more. He leaned in, his slate eyes storming with unspoken intent. I clutched my bleeding wrist. Something was still not right. Pain ripped through my arms—I shrieked, dropping them to the floor.

"It's not enough, Nora." Landan leaned closer, his nose an inch from mine. His hands braced the floor beside me. "It's not enough." He seized my head, his thumbs digging into my temples. Light flashed, and suddenly, I was Moira, plummeting toward the rocks at the base of the cliff.

"I WANT TO LIVE!" The high-pitched scream tore from my throat as I braced for the shattering impact.

24

Great-Gran's Sin

I gasped, finding myself back on the bench within the light. The white fog was a welcome reprieve from the darkness on the other side. My eyes widened as I caught my breath. I turned to Landan. "It didn't do anything?" I cried. "Help me."

"It did do somethin', Nora. But this is only goin' ta get harder. Ya aren't finished."

"What do you mean—*harder?*" I gaped at him. The tide had already pulled me under; I had nothing left to fight with.

"Poison must be siphoned."

My chin trembled. "What else am I supposed to do?"

"Ya have ta forgive them all."

"All? All who?"

He nodded. "Those whose damage has left this curse for ya."

I dropped my head. "My family?"

"All of them."

"Okay." My breath hitched, tears filling my eyes. I dove in with all the sincerity I could muster. "I forgive Mom."

Light flashed. Pain like a thousand needles pierced my veins.

Green mist coiled over my fingers, searing my skin like acid. The anger I harbored toward my mom clawed to the surface—anger for leaving, for dying, for being too busy before she left me behind. But I meant it. I didn't want to carry that resentment any longer.

My bones flared as if splintering under the pressure.

"Ow," I cried, holding myself.

"Don't stop." Landan squeezed my hand, his voice a steady anchor.

"I forgive my gran and Aunt Neive."

My heart throbbed. My skin was on fire. I arced my back against the pain. But I meant it. I didn't blame them. I understood them. But a flare erupted—resistance toward my gran. She hadn't protected me. Not really. She'd only left me afraid, alone, and in the dark. Sobs shook my body as I wailed, "I love you, Gran."

And my grandad. He'd never hurt me. His smile was still a fond memory, even in his silence. My mom's resentment for him was not something I wanted. I let him go too.

My own voice—raw, like I'd been screaming—seared my ears. Wind swirled around me, lifting me from the floor. My body contorted backward, rending with pain. Black feathers surrounded me. My name, *N-O-R-A*, swirled with the cawing chaos of wings. The furniture crashed into the walls.

Landan held no remorse for me. Not this Landan—not the one with the gray eyes. He tilted his head forward, and his eyes dipped into shadow. He wasn't my friend. He was about to let me die.

"Yer hurting me." I dug my nails into the wood bench.

"I'm sorry, Nora," Landan whispered. "Ya can't stop. Ya have ta finish it."

Only one person remained. My great-grandad. "I can't forgive him."

"Ya have ta? If ya don't, then the curse will have its way."

"But he killed you, Landan. He was a drunk. He hurt your mom, and your sisters."

"This is true," Landan growled. His face flashed back to the Landan without love in his dark eyes, whose menacing brow hooded his eyes. "But it was my mother, Moira, who has done more damage wit' her hate than *he* ever did wit' his drink. Her *unforgiveness* is what damned us all."

I shook my head. "But he doesn't deserve it."

The white sanctuary melted away as Landan's steel glare deepened like claws into my flesh. "It isn't about what he deserves. Don't ya want ta be released from this *bondage*? Ya can't hold hatred toward him and hope it won't hurt ya. It doesn't work that way, Nora. It will only kill ya."

The wind stopped swirling. I plummeted to the floor. The concussive noise calmed. No crows in sight. My hands bled from the glass. Lacerations on my cheeks stung. Landan stood in front of me in the dark. His head and shoulders drooped in a motionless stance.

Fear clamped my throat, but I fought it down. "L-Landan?"

He didn't move. The house was wrecked, like a cyclone had torn through it. I slid one leg under me. Glass shifted beneath my foot. I kept my eye on Landan. His eerie frame was all too still. My pulse pounded, a frantic drum in my ears. I lifted my second foot, fearful that even the slightest movement would rouse him.

I breathed a slow sigh, strengthening myself.

I know what I need to do.

I would release my great-grandad, but not just him. Great-Gran had done all this. If it weren't for her, Declan would be by my side. All the women in my family would still be alive. Forgiving my great-grandad became easier and easier in light of what Moira had chosen to do to us all. But—

I won't take what she's done any further into my life.

"Landan?" I gulped, swallowing down a lump of apprehension. I took a careful step toward him. He remained still. "I'm going to let him go. And, Moira. I for—"

Landan's wings shifted. He burst before me in a flash. His hand clutched my throat, squeezing. Terror seized me as I fought for breath—fought to speak. My nails tore at his hands, desperate to free myself.

Landan's teeth clenched—hate pierced through his menacing glare. Rasps escaped my throat as he lifted me from the floor. I thrashed in his grip, kicking my feet against his legs. The edges of my vision blurred. Landan's thick and suffocating hold was merciless. My awareness slipped away.

Desperate moments faded like my consciousness. The flicker of his dark wings stole away my last hope. I tried to mouth my forgiveness, but my eyes rolled back in my head.

The thought of my great-gran's choice—the moment her fury had caused her to hate—bled through my mind like hot, blistering acid. Her scream as she realized her son was dead rang in my head. Her fists beating her husband's back flared like bitter, hammering bolts. Her desolate agony weighed heavy like a stone in my palm. In my mind's eye, I clutched the cold, hateful thing tight, held it over the cliff beyond the edge of The Flaherty House, and—

I let it go. It fell, tumbling further and further, until the effervescing sea swallowed it forever.

It was gone.

Right there, at the edge of the cliff, I was free. Laughter poured from my lips. Tears streamed down my cheeks. I hadn't wanted this burden. I hadn't asked for it. But it had been there nonetheless, all my life—like a long cord attaching to a past I hadn't lived. And now, it was gone. It was as if I could fly.

Landan's grip loosened. I dropped to the floor like a load of bricks. I coughed, hand to my throat, inhaling air into my lungs. Blood rushed into my head. I heaved, "I forgive her, Landan. It's . . . done."

I gazed up at him. His hand still hovered above me.

"And"—I rasped, still sucking in breath—"I forgive you. I forgive you."

25

Fire!

My head buzzed, and spots dotted my vision like static on a television. Landan knelt in front of me, gripping my shoulders.

"Nora!" His voice sounded strange—distant.

My body was heavy. I couldn't hold my head up anymore. The whole world turned sideways as my head hit the floor.

Landan's face hovered above mine. His eyes were green like the sea. Then everything fell black.

The discordant shrill of seagulls calling across the shore filtered through my ears. Cold wind brushed my cheeks. I curled into a ball, pain stinging my arms and cheeks. My throat was raw when I swallowed.

My body lay on something cold, but a soft surface cradled my head. I cracked my eyes open. The pre-dawn horizon of the sea met my gaze. Memories surged of leaving Declan behind, the curse coming for me, and Landan. My breath hitched, and I leapt to my feet.

The world spun. I stumbled, but someone's hands caught me.

"Careful now."

Landan. He held me steady. His eyes were bright and his face soft. Oh, how I wished it was Declan.

I turned away. I'd been lying on my grandad's bench—the house right behind it. All the windows were shattered, leaving only jagged glass remnants behind like sharp teeth.

"I—I moved ya. I didn't t'ink it would be good for ya ta lay in all that glass."

Urgency spun me toward the trail leading to the shore. "We need to—"

I stopped. I barely recognized my own voice—it was hoarse, scratchy. "De—Declan." Hope flickered, and I chased it like a moth to a dying flame, desperate to go after him.

"I t'ink ya need ta rest." Landan pulled me toward the bench to sit back down. I let him. Everything still swirled in my head. "I'm sorry, Nora. For everyt'ing."

"Did we do it?" I asked him. "Is the curse destroyed?"

"You did it, Nora. No one else will suffer from me ma's witchcraft."

My brows pressed tight. The pieces scattered too fast for me to catch. I just needed to find Declan. I looked up at Landan, who stood in front of me. His eyes were brilliant, soft as the sky tinged with lavender hues.

"Y-You bore this curse all these years. Now you're free, too. I can see it in your eyes."

The wind flailed his hair in front of his eyes. His peacoat furled like a cape, exposing the white buttoned-up shirt and gray slacks. Were his clothes always this old fashioned?

"I need to go to Declan."

"You won't need ta," he said, holding out his hand.

"But—"

I gasped. Orange flickers lit Landan's hand, a remorseful grin curled his lips. His fingers glowed yellow, then began dissipating into sparks on the wind, like a hot wick being blown out.

"Landan!" I jumped to my feet. "What's happening?"

"Someone's burnin' the cursed bones."

"Declan! Is he okay?" My heart burst, and my hands flew to my mouth. Tears formed in my eyes. I stepped toward the trail, ready to run for him, but found myself turning back. Landan's arms were now a whirl of glimmering flares, encircling him. Fire bloomed at his feet. "Oh, my God, Landan! I need to stop it."

"No." Landan shook his head. A peaceful acceptance brimmed in his eyes. "It's too late. Besides, now it's done—time for it all ta be burned."

I ran to him but stood back, unable to touch him as the orange tendrils whirled up his legs. "I don't want you to go." Sparks swirled around me.

His stare floated gently over my face.

He's ready to go.

I cried, "Thank you, Landan, for being with me all these years. For helping me, even when I didn't understand. Maybe even when I didn't deserve it."

"You were worth it." His words were steady, his gaze alight and unwavering. There wasn't a single tear or sign of worry. He seemed to welcome the moment to finally move on. "Thank you for not burnin' those bones so I could be here ta help ya."

He faded fast. My fingers reached to caress his cheek. They filtered through him like he wasn't there—and then—he was gone. Orange sparks floated away, like a flurry of fireflies on the wind, until they vanished.

Tinges of deep orange now melded with the dark sky. Tears pricked behind my eyes, pressing for release, but I blinked hard and straightened my spine.

Seems a shame to fall to pieces.

Landan had just been set free. He wasn't meant to stay—he needed to move on.

More sparks brushed past me. More and more, and then the rush of a fiery roar. I spun around. Flames burst from the windows of my grandparents' old bedroom. Roaring plumes billowed into the sky. My mouth fell open, but my legs carried me forward. Flames consumed the inside of the house through the living room window.

All I could do was stare. The inferno blazed hotter. The heat permeated the air in rippling waves. Wind blew gusts of smoke around my face. The bitter scent of charred debris stung my nose. Yet, even in the wild acrid air, a peaceful steadiness settled over me, as if the loss somehow atoned for itself as all that remained burned away.

Footsteps scraped the gravel behind me. I tore my eyes from the flames and turned. Declan stood at the trailhead. My chest pumped, and my chin quivered. Blood stained the side of his face and ear below his temple. His shoulders heaved with apparent exhaustion but stilled as he stared wide-eyed at the burning house. His face paled, but when his gaze locked on me, he gripped his chest.

I opened my mouth to scream his name but no sound emerged. My feet stumbled forward, carrying me to Declan. My hands reached for him, desperate to touch him—to confirm he was real. I crashed into his arms, my body molding to his as he clutched me in his embrace. I pressed my face against his chest. His racing heartbeat was music to my ears.

He cupped my face in his palms. Tears hovered in his eyes, spilling over as a shaky smile spread across his face.

He tsked, sliding his fingers over my cheek. "What are we goin' ta do about ya bleedin' all the time?" He brushed his lips against my forehead and pulled me into a tight embrace.

I buried my sobs against his chest. "I thought you were dead."

He chuckled like he couldn't fathom the truth either. "Ya, I might've been lucky on this one." He pulled me back again and looked at me. "I t'ought I might have lost ya as well. When I woke up on the beach, and you were gone"—tears splashed from his eyes—"all I could t'ink of was gettin' that curse burnin'."

"Landan helped me."

Declan's brows crimped. "Look at ya. Cuts on yer cheeks, black on yer forehead." His eyes darted. "Where is Landan? What about the curse?"

"It's over, Dec. It's done, and—Landan's gone."

His lips thinned, and his eyes narrowed. A quiet moment passed between us before Declan's features softened. "Are ya a'right?"

"Honestly?" I grinned. "I think I am. I really, really am."

"What are we goin' ta do about the fire?"

I turned back toward the burning house. The siding was blackened. Flames now consumed the exterior, as well as the interior. I sighed. "Just let it burn."

Declan pulled his phone from his back pocket and dialed 999. He held the phone to his ear and waited. "Yes. We have a fire at The Flaherty House, at 23 Shorline Way . . . ya . . . no, everybody's out . . . the whole house . . . ya . . . we might also need some medical help . . ."

His conversation with the emergency operator faded to the background. The orange roaring flames held no more trauma. For nearly the entirety of my life, there had been this invisible threat. Whether it was the darkness outside my window, or Declan and I being torn apart, it had always been there, and now it was gone.

I could dream. No one was coming for me. No one was going to take me from Declan. My hands, which once clenched everything so tightly, now hung free by my sides.

The grinding of tires over gravel stole my attention. A

white Volkswagen pulled into the drive, sliding to a halt. Lem stepped out of the driver's side, and his eyes widened.

"Dear Mary and Joseph." Lem threw his hands over his head. "Declan! What's happened?"

Lem rushed to me and touched my arm. "I'm okay," I said.

"Good Lord, Nora." His eyes bounced over me, and he winced.

I must look like a mess.

"Ya aren't okay." Lem gasped, clearly noticing the blood on his son's face.

"I'm okay, Da. The fire brigade is on the way."

Lem rushed over to Declan and embraced his son.

The passenger door opened.

My heart dropped when, instead of Della or Patty, a man with deep brown hair and a bearded chin emerged.

Dad!

26

What Remains

ad stood behind the open car door. His shoulders sagged, and his eyes seemed to flicker with unspoken regret. Seeing him should've rattled me, but it didn't. I couldn't explain it. I turned back toward the burning house, the roar drowning out the last vestiges of pain.

Dad's slow, yet steady footfalls crunched the ground until he reached me. Part of me wanted to walk away, the sting of old resentment still smoldering. But another part held me there, rooted in the quiet shift that had already taken place. My perspective had changed. Ashes drifted through the air, soft reminders that peace would never be found in my scorn.

My dad gaped at the flames, then turned toward me, working his jaw as if he wasn't sure where to begin. "Lem called me. And . . . and there was the charge on my credit card."

I gave no reply. I figured as much. I wasn't mad. I stood there, waiting for the right emotion to find me, but nothing came—I just kept staring into the flames. "I . . . I'm sorry about the house. I hope you had insurance."

"I'm just glad you're okay. What happened?"

"I, um . . . hard to explain. I didn't start the fire. I just—I broke the curse."

My dad's jaw dropped. "How did you . . . How did you know about—"

"I just wish"—emotions surged up my throat—"I'd done it before we lost Mom. I could've saved her." I still couldn't bring myself to look at him. Not yet. I was the one holding onto the wall between us.

Why am I doing this?

My chin trembled. "I'm so—"

"I'm so sorry, Nora." A sob caught in my dad's throat. "I'm sorry for—for everything. I . . . I love you."

I couldn't hold back any longer. "I'm sorry too," I burst, crashing into his arms. I hadn't hugged my dad in years. I'd forgotten what it felt like. His strong, warm arms squeezed me, pushing back the dross of so many lost years. "I didn't mean those things I said to you. I don't want to be angry at you anymore."

He squeezed me tighter and cried like heavy weights fell off him too.

I'd never heard my dad cry before. I'd never even seen a tear in his eye, except for the *one* he'd shed at Mom's funeral. Pain seemed to escape through each of his sobs, mingled with spasms of relief-filled laughter.

Like Landan said, the poison had to be siphoned. Once it was out, something new, healthy, and clean could take its place. Perhaps my dad had forgiven me too.

He held me back to look at me. His moist, red eyes sparkled with repentance. "I, uh . . . I know things have been hard between us." He sniffed. "But when you come back to Chicago, I know things will be—"

"Dad." I shook my head, squeezing his sleeve. "I'm staying here—with Declan." Declan's hand found mine. "I'm not going to go back with you."

Dad's eyes dropped to the ground. "What about school?"

"I don't know."

My dad nodded, pulling a hanky from his back pocket and wiping his face. He cleared his throat. "Of course. I'm sorry"—he clasped Declan's shoulder—"that I ever tore you two apart. I didn't realize the impact it would have. I kept waiting for Nora to get over the move and adjust." He tsked. "Never happened."

Declan nodded, his mouth twisting, his eyes awash with emotion.

"I guess neither did you," he said to Declan. "Your dad and I had a lot to talk about before he brought me here." He glanced over at Lem. "Set me straight on a few things. I don't think any of us realized how significant a bond you two had."

I couldn't believe my ears. This was the first time my dad admitted to his faults, or even showed a care about anybody he'd hurt.

Dad paused, scanning the fire. "It seems to me there were solutions, though drastic, that Una and I didn't know we had. Looking at this." He motioned to the burning house. "I still think I would've made the same choice."

My dad cupped my cheek, running his thumb over a cut, and whispered, "Only a fighter like you could have done it. I'm not going to force you to do anything you don't want to anymore, Nora. I've learned my lesson."

More tears welled in my eyes. Maybe I hadn't given my dad enough credit. Or, maybe we both had lessons we needed to learn.

Declan beamed next to me, as if saying, *"I told ya so."*

The sirens roared closer. Soon, the flashing red lights of the fire brigade blazed up the drive, followed by an ambulance. The chaos of paramedics pulled us all apart. One of the paramedics, a woman, wrapped a blanket around my shoulders. A quiet warmth settled into my chest. It was as though I'd been swimming in a sea of ice. She escorted me to sit on the open end of the ambulance. A flashlight danced in my eyes. The other paramedic sat Declan beside me. I sighed in relief as she prodded my neck with her fingers. I hissed at the soreness. Another paramedic checked Declan's eyes.

Fire hoses doused water over the flames. Nothing but black char would remain. Luckily, I had my gran's mug in Declan's car, but honestly, everything else needed to fade into the history that held no power over me anymore.

The paramedics decided Declan and I needed a little more *TLC* at the clinic. I would need stitches on a few of the deeper cuts on my hands from the glass, and they were worried about Declan's possible concussion.

We pulled away. The firefighters still fought the flames, their silhouettes growing smaller through the tiny ambulance windows. I peered over at Declan, who sat across from me. He smiled, his head bobbing with the rolling of the vehicle. I ran my hand over my pocket. The whelk shell was still there, just like Declan.

I would never be the same. I grinned back at him. Fond memories danced in my head. The bitter ones faded, and I no longer wished for what I didn't have.

"Declan, how are you going to explain all this to your dad?"

He shrugged. "I'll figure that out later. Besides, me da's lack of shock tells me he might know somet'in' more about all this than he let on. What's most important now, anyways, is that ya did it." His steady voice brimmed with certainty. "I told ya you were a fighter."

I huffed, rolling my eyes. I guess he was right. Every small choice had led me here. Like Great-Gran, I had to choose.

And I chose. I chose Declan. I chose my dad too. But most of all, I chose to forgive.

Declan's smile grew even wider as his eyes stayed on mine.

My cheeks flushed. "What?" I giggled.

"Just so ya know—I'm goin' ta ask ya ta marry me some day, Nora Morrigan."

A wave of giddy happiness washed over me. "I'm worried

about your head, Dec. Are you sure that concussion isn't doing the talking?"

"No." His expression turned serious—his voice unwavering. "I'm not lettin' ya go from me again."

Epilogue

I did stay in Carraig Brón, at least for a couple more months. My dad did too. He and I still had a lot to work through—our relationship had its gaps, and trust was still something we needed to build. But we were both trying. And now that I no longer looked at him through the lens of blame, things would be easier. He was able to connect with my mom's memory through the people there, and I got to spend more time with Declan, uninterrupted by all the chaos I'd arrived in.

My dad and I stayed in the rooms at Pete's Inn & Pub. Both Don and Carla seemed more than happy that we stayed with them. On Christmas, Carla and my dad sat shoulder to shoulder, on Lem and Patty's sofa, looking at old pictures of Mom. They cried, laughed, and ate plenty of Christmas cake and custard.

I hated to leave, but I did return to school after the holidays. And that was after Declan got down on one knee and asked me to marry him, just as he said he would. That was a hard, fast yes from me. I couldn't believe it. Della seemed even happier than we were, practically knocking us both over when I'd said yes.

My dad also surprised us. He would use the insurance money to rebuild The Flaherty House—for Mom. She had loved that place, and the emptiness left behind felt wrong. The rebuild would take time, but he gave it to Declan and me, a home for after we married.

"It would make your mom happy," he said.

And I was too.

Don and Carla even reconsidered selling Pete's in all the happiness. Instead, they struck a deal with Lem and Declan to become partners, allowing them to buy a small place in the city closer to their kids and spend less time running the place. Don promised to give Declan his secret spice recipe for the chips.

I was right—sugar was one of the ingredients.

Declan's brain flooded with ideas on how to make the pub more modern.

Lem let Declan take over the pub, while he and Della remained at the post and café. There was a little sadness in Lem, letting Declan go from the family business into his own. The partnership with Don was more for Declan than Lem. But it was quite the reward the way Declan beamed about it.

Declan only had a semester to go until he finished school. I still had the rest of the year, but then I would be back. My dad was eager to return to Chicago and start working again.

Summer plans for a wedding were in bloom before Christmas had even ended. Della, Patty, and Carla had it all handled. I didn't mind. It helped me miss my mom a little less, and I wasn't savvy with planning a wedding, anyway.

I wished my mom and Gran—even Landan—could be there. But all I really cared about was that I would get to spend the rest of my life with Declan in the place I loved most. The curse was broken, and my family was set free to build a history—maybe even a legacy, however simple—that would be like a tree with branches for my children's children to swing on.

THE END.

Acknowledgments

I want to thank my sister, *Amanda Booth*, who is always the first to uncover my hidden gems. The time we spent reminiscing about Grandma and sharing stories of Copco Lake is etched into every page of this book.

To my ride-or-die author friend, co-conspirator, podcast partner, and editor, *Stephanie Cotta*—I wouldn't want to walk this path without you.

To *Brae and Jill Wyckoff*: "This is all your fault." Thank you for being among the first to believe in me as a storyteller.

To my *husband and kids*: you are, and always will be, my greatest source of strength and encouragement.

Brielle—I'll always remember this as the first book of mine you read. Sharing my inner world with you for the first time meant more than words can say. I hope you tell stories and create beyond anything I ever could.

And finally, thank you to *Sherry Ward, Square Tree Publishing,* and *Imagine Now Publishing* for being an essential part of bringing my books into the world.

More From Angela R. Hughes

THE ONCE & FUTURE CHRONICLES

BOOK 1: ELANOR & THE SONG OF THE BARD
BOOK 2: MERLIN & THE MAGIC OF TIME
BOOK 3: ARTHUR & THE GOLDEN DRAGON

THE ILLYDS OF PRYDAIN'S HEROES

THE LOST SON OF ORCADES - PART 1
THE LOST SON OF ORCADES - PART 2
COMING SOON!

**Find these books at AMAZON.com or
wherever books are sold.**

For More Information
www.angelarhughes.com

About the Author

Angela R. Hughes is a historical fantasy author based in Waco, Texas. Her ambition is to write stories that grip and inspire readers, alluring them into her fascinating world of myth and legend.

Angela believes in the power of dynamic, inspired storytelling. She has always been intrigued by folklore and legend, and desired to create her own. Particularly drawn to Arthurian legend and its ancient roots in the history of the Cymraeg (Welsh) people, she has extensively studied Arthurian legend and Celtic mythology.

Much of her fascination with the Celtic world began during her time living in Ireland, where she fell in love with the history and landscapes of Ireland, Wales, Scotland, and England.

In addition to writing, Angela spends her time researching ancient histories and languages—which led her to learn to speak the Welsh language. She also enjoys chatting with fellow fantasy nerds on the podcast she co-hosts, THE INK MAGES, available on YouTube and Spotify.

The Once and Future Chronicles Trilogy is the first of her published works. She is currently working on, *The Lost Son of Orcadés Part 1 & 2*, the first two books in *The Illyds of Prydain's Heroes Series*.

Learn more about Angela's books by visiting www.angelar-hughes.com. You are also invited to follow her author journey on Facebook, Instagram, TikTok and Amazon.

Let's be Legendary!

Instagram/TikTok: @angela.r.hughes
Facebook: Angela R. Hughes @onceandfuturechronicles
Twitter: @ARHughesAuthor

If you enjoyed this book, I'd be so grateful if you'd
Write A Review....

It's easy and helps my book get into the hands of
more readers.

Step 1: Go To www.AMAZON.com
Step 2: Search for my book in Amazon books
Step 3: Scroll down to REVIEWS
Step 4: Leave a Review

I'd love to know your thoughts about my book.
Contact me at *angelarhuges.mythiclegends@gmail.com*
Let me know what you got out of the book.
Join my newsletter for more info on events and releases.
Sign up here: www.angelarhughes.com

Thank You for Your Support!